EXES AND O'S

What Reviewers Say About Joy Argento's Work

Before Now

"*Before Now* by Joy Argento is a mixture of modern day romance and historical fiction. …There was some welcome humour and a bit of angst. An interesting story well told."—*Kitty Kat's Book Review Blog*

Emily's Art and Soul

"…the leads are well rounded and credible. As a 'friends to lovers' romance the author skillfully transforms their budding friendship to an increasing intimacy. Mindy, Emily's Down syndrome sister, is a great secondary character, very realistic in her traits and interactions with other people. Her fresh outlook on life and her 'best friend' declarations help to keep the upbeat tone."—*LezReviewBooks*

"This was such a sweet book. Great story that would be perfect as a holiday read. The plot was fun and the pace really good. The protagonists were enjoyable and Emily's character was well fleshed out. …This is the first book I've read by Joy Argento and it won't be the last. I'm looking forward to what comes next." —*Rainbow Literary Society*

Visit us at www.boldstrokesbooks.com

By the Author

Emily's Art and Soul

Before Now

No Regrets

Carrie and Hope

Exes and O's

EXES AND O'S

by

Joy Argento

2022

EXES AND O'S

ISBN 13: 978-1-63679-017-6

This Trade Paperback Original Is Published By
Bold Strokes Books, Inc.
P.O. Box 249
Valley Falls, NY 12185

First Edition: January 2022

CREDITS
Editor: Cindy Cresap
Production Design: Susan Ramundo
Cover Design By Tammy Seidick and Joy Argento

Acknowledgments

Special thanks to my editor, Cindy Cresap, for all your help. I have learned so much from you.

Thanks to Sandy and all the great people at Bold Strokes Books. I am so happy to be part of this family.

Thanks to anyone who took a chance on me and bought this or any of my books. I appreciate you more than you will ever know. Read on!

As always thank you to my family, my kids, grandkids, and siblings for your support and love.

Dedication

This book is dedicated to Lea Caruso.
I will miss you forever.

CHAPTER ONE

"Oh," Ali Daniels said to Charley, her best friend since freshman year in college. "Oh, yeah. That's a great idea." But did she really have the nerve to track down her exes, interview them, and ask them what she had done wrong in their relationships? You bet she did. At least in that moment she thought so. Of course, the three drinks she'd just had may have played a part in her confidence. Tequila was known to do that.

"What's the plan? How are you going to do this?" Charley asked.

"Well, the main objective is to find out why the relationship didn't last. Right? Seems like everyone breaks up with me. I'm not the one to do the leaving," Ali said. That had been the case with her most recent breakup. She and April had only been together for three months when April announced that they were through. Ali thought it had been going well—well enough, anyway. Nothing was perfect. She chose to overlook their differences. Apparently, April wasn't so willing to do the same.

"Let's make a list of all your ex-girlfriends. It shouldn't be too hard to track them down on the internet. Then we'll make a list of the questions you should ask them." Charley ran a hand over his long hair. His latest dye job turned the strands a rich shade of purple, with hot pink highlights. Ali thought Charley's constant hair color change was a bit immature for his age. She would have thought he would have stopped that by the time he turned thirty-eight. At the same time she envied the fact that Charley had enough self-confidence to do it. Charley often referred to himself as a triple bypass. Biracial. Bisexual. Binary. He felt both male and female at different times, sometimes both at the same time—his definition. He would have added bipartisan, but he leaned too far to the Left for that.

Ali often felt more comfortable blending into the woodwork than standing out. Maybe that's why she decided to be a writer. She could hide behind her computer to write and still have fame and fortune. Sometimes her name was recognized, but never her face. Her choice to leave her picture off the back of her books had been a good one. Ali was one of the lucky ones. When her third novel hit the *New York Times* Best Seller list, she was able to quit her job as a proofreader and focus on her writing, earning enough money to live comfortably.

"Where can I find a pad of paper and a pen?" Charley set his half-finished drink on the coffee table.

"My desk in the office. Top drawer." Ali sat on the floor, cross-legged with her back propped up against her secondhand couch. It wasn't that she couldn't afford a new one. She could afford several if she wanted them. But this one still looked nice and was uber comfortable, so why bother replacing what was working. That might be a metaphor for her relationships, she realized. If nothing major was wrong, why throw it away?

Her apartment sported three bedrooms, one for sleeping, one for guests—mostly Charley when he had too much to drink, and occasionally her parents—and one for an office. That's were Ali did most of her writing.

"Got it." Charley waved the pad in the air like he had won a prize. He handed it to Ali. "Start with your most recent breakup and work your way backward."

Ali shook her head. Doubts crept in. Did she really want to face April and her other exes, even if it was only in writing? Charley grabbed Ali's glass and made her another drink. Two sips of the fresh margarita, and Ali began to write. She ended up with seven names.

Charley took the list and looked it over. "Um, you seem to be missing one."

Ali took a large sip of her drink, running her tongue along the edge of the glass to get more of the salt. "Who?"

"Your high school girl friend? What was her name again? Maggie? Marley? M something." Charley handed the paper back to Ali.

Ali shook her head. "No. I don't need to include her. I know what went wrong there."

"I'm thinking *nooo*." Charley stretched the word out like it had more than one syllable. "You definitely need to include her. After all, hindsight is fifty-fifty."

"I thought hindsight was twenty-twenty?"

"Not in this case, honey. This information is worth way more than twenty." He waved his *fuck me* red polished fingernails at the paper in Ali's hand. "Write down what's-her-name—the high school chick."

The last thing Ali wanted was to contact Madison Parker again. The girl pretty enough to be a model, with the name that matched, head cheerleader and all, was in her past, and Ali wanted to keep it that way. She had thought about her through the years, of course. Wondered where she was and what she was doing. Was she happy? Had she left that small town in Maryland like Ali had? College had changed things for Ali. She decided to stay in Central New York after attending Syracuse University. Syracuse wasn't a huge city, but it sure was bigger than Clyde, Maryland, whose only claim to fame was being an hour from the beach. That and the fact that the Clyde High School football team won the state championship three years in a row. "Why?" Ali asked.

"Child, I know how important she was to you. You've talked about her enough times." Had she? She probably did without even realizing she was doing it.

Madison Parker. The girl who broke Ali's heart twenty years ago. She should have been long forgotten, but for some reason she still took up space in Ali's head and sometimes even managed to ping Ali's heart. "I know why that didn't work."

"So? Have you talked to her about it?"

Talk to her about it? No. No need for that. Her own eyes had told her everything she needed to know. She shook her head without explaining.

"Ali, add her to the list." It was more of a demand than a suggestion.

Ali knew it was no use arguing with Charley. "Whatever. Fine," she said.

"We need a list of questions. Any idea what you want to ask your exes?"

"I would like to know why they were stupid enough to break up with me?"

Charley laughed. "That might not be the best opening question." He grabbed the pad of paper, turned it over, and made a list.

1. Did you ever love me?
2. At any point, did you see yourself spending forever with me?
3. If yes, what changed?
4. Did I ever do anything that made you jealous?
5. What's your biggest regret about our relationship?
6. What's the worst thing you think I did?
7. What did you think of my friends?
8. What's your favorite memory of us being together?
9. What was your favorite thing about me?

10. What was your least favorite thing about me?
11. Did we have a good sex life?
12. What should I have done differently?
13. Do you wish we could have worked it out?
14. If you could tell me anything, what would you say?
15. Do you ever wish we were still together?

He handed the list to Ali. Ali crossed off three of the questions. "I really don't want to know what any of them thought of my friends—aka you."

"Hey."

Ali smirked. "Don't worry. I know they all loved you. Well, at least the ones that met you. Some of these relationships were pretty short. What do you think would qualify as a relationship? More than three dates? More than a month?"

"I think anyone you were exclusive with as long as you slept with them. What other questions did you cross off?"

Ali read off the paper. "What's your favorite memory of us being together and what was your favorite thing about me. Those sound like I'm fishing for compliments."

Charley finished his drink. "I think you should leave those in. You want to know the stuff they liked as well as the stuff they didn't. How else are you going to learn what you were doing right?"

"Maybe you've got a point." Ali looked at the list of names again and crossed off a couple. "I don't think these two qualify as relationships under your definition."

"Let's go on Facebook and see who we can find. I want you to message them before you sober up and change your mind."

Ali laughed. "So, you want me to *drunk*-message them? That might not be the best idea."

"Yes, it's fine," Charley said. "We have the list of questions. You can come up with an opening explanation for why you want to know. If we stick to the script, you'll be fine. You are a writer after all. You'll think of something."

He stood, pulled Ali to her feet, and led the way to Ali's office and her computer. It was a modest room as far as workspaces went. A desk with a hutch sat against one wall, complete with a comfortable, well-worn office chair. There was a fairly new recliner in the corner that Ali occasionally used, Macbook on her lap, when she wrote. A small bookcase rounded out the sparse furnishings. A thesaurus and several reference books littered the shelves. Ali rarely used them, preferring the internet for her research.

It took Ali several minutes to write what she thought was a good opening explanation for the questions. They were able to find four of the five women on the list on Facebook. The only one they couldn't find was Madison. A Google search listed her as the owner of a business called O's in their hometown of Clyde.

"Guess she didn't stray too far from home," Ali said. And why should she? She seemed to have found what she wanted there. The memory, seared into Ali's memory, had left a large burn hole in her heart.

"What's O's? A sex shop specializing in orgasms?"

Ali spit out a mouthful of her drink trying to control her laughter. "Not likely. Not in that dead little town."

"Well, whatever it is, there's an address. Let's see what you came up with for an opening statement."

"You make it sound like we're going to court."

"That makes sense. In a way you are on trial here."

Ali moved aside so Charley could see the computer.

Hi,

I know we haven't spoken in a while. I hope you are doing well. I am working on self-improvement, trying to become a better person and thus a better partner in a relationship. I'm hoping

you can help me out by answering some questions for me. I would really appreciate it. Yours truly,
    Ali (your ex)
    AliB@mailbox.com

"Perfect. Now send a copy to each one."

Ali hesitated. Drunk or not, this probably wasn't a good idea. She should just give up trying to find a lasting relationship altogether. They never ended well, and she always ended up alone. It would probably be better just to stay that way.

"Do it. Private message them. I really think it will help, honey. I want you to be able to find happiness."

"I'm not going to find happiness with someone else if I can't find it in me."

"I know that. I'm glad you know it. But if you learn more about yourself, then maybe you can figure out the happiness part."

"You really think this will help?"

"Honey, I really do."

"I hope you're right." Ali did as she was told, cringing each time she hit *send*.

"Now for Madison Parker. Print out a copy. We have no choice but to mail it," Charley told her.

"But I know—"

"Just do it. I promise you won't regret it."

"So, you're a psychic now?"

"Always have been, darling." Charley grabbed the sheet of paper as soon as it was done printing. "Envelopes?"

Ali didn't answer. Charley opened two desk drawers before finding them. He inserted the printed sheet, addressed the envelope to Madison at O's, found stamps in the same drawer, and headed out of the office with it.

"Hey," Ali sputtered.

"I'm going to drop this in the outgoing letter box before you have a chance to change your mind." He disappeared out the door. She could hear the apartment door open and close and open again moments later. Charley reappeared. "Done."

The computer let out a *ding* indicating there was a new Facebook message. It was from April.

"Wow. That was fast. What does it say?" Charley asked, even though he was already reading it over her shoulder.

Seriously, Ali, if you have questions like this then you have issues. I told you everything I thought about you when we broke up. Move the fuck on.

"Huh. That's not helpful," Ali said. "Or nice."

"What did she say when she broke up with you? Anything useful for your next relationship?"

Ali thought for a moment. "She said she'd had about enough of me and my crazy ways when I wouldn't let her kill a spider in her apartment. I used the teacup she'd inherited from her grandmother to capture it and take it outside. It wasn't like I broke the cup or anything."

"That's not worth breaking up over. Did she say anything else?"

Ali shook her head. She was having trouble remembering any conversations they had had. Seemed like sex was their main event.

"What did you see in that girl anyway? I thought she was kind of a bitch?"

Again, Ali was at a loss. What had she seen in April? April was a strong personality. She dominated the relationship, and everything had to be her way. The one time Ali had gone against her wishes she was sent packing. Maybe bitch *was* the right word for her. "Damned if I know."

Charley looked at her and shook his head.

"What?" Ali asked.

"You know," he said, holding up the list of exes Ali had made. "I'm starting to see a pattern here." He handed Ali the list. "Tell me what you liked about any of these women?"

Ali looked it over. "Brenda. Hmm. Brenda had a nice smile."

"I remember Brenda. How many times did she actually smile at you?"

"All the time—the first few weeks." Ali hadn't realized that her kindness didn't seem to extend beyond that.

Charley unbuttoned the top button on his plain cotton shirt. It was much less feminine than the way he usually dressed. He would have at least three buttons undone before the evening was over. Alcohol tended to cause him to overheat. "Anything else?"

"The sex was good," Ali said. Although it had always been on Brenda's terms, when and where and even *how* they were intimate. Ali tapped her chin. There didn't seem to be anything else she liked about Brenda.

"And how long were you with her?"

"Eight months. She broke up with me through a text."

"So, a short-lived smile and decent sex was all she offered you and you stayed for eight months?"

Ali shrugged. She wasn't liking this conversation. "Screw her," she said.

"You've already done that, and from what you've said you liked it."

"Ha ha. Not funny."

A loud ding announced another Facebook message. Ali jumped.

"Guess they can't wait to tell me what's wrong with me," Ali said. "I don't like this game."

"It's not a game, baby. It's a learning experience. So far we've learned that some of the women you've been with aren't very nice people." Charley leaned over her shoulder, grabbed the mouse, and clicked on the message. "It's from Janet. Let's hope she's a little nicer than April was. Let's see…" He scrolled down reading out loud. "Did you ever love me? She said no. At any point, did you see yourself spending forever with me? No again. No to her ever being jealous."

"This is torture. Do we really have to do this?" Ali interrupted him.

"Hun, this is important. Now, where was I?" He scrolled farther down. "No regrets. Oh, listen to this."

Ali put her face in her hands, lowered her head to her desk, and banged it against the wood a few times.

"The question was—what's the worst thing you think I did."

"Do I really want to know?" Ali's voice was muffled against her hands.

Charley didn't miss a beat. "There wasn't anything you did that was bad. In fact you were too good. Or maybe I should say too mild. You never demanded or really even asked for anything. You just went along with whatever I wanted. You bent over backwards to make me happy. You and I were never right together, but you didn't seem to notice that."

Ali picked her head up from the desk and brushed a few strands of hair out of her eyes. "What. The worse thing I did was try to make her happy?"

Charley stood and put his hands on his hips. "You are missing the point here." He shook his head.

"What's the point then? What am I missing?"

"You didn't even consider yourself in that relationship. She makes it sound like you were beating a dead horse. Like you were chasing after something that was never going to work." He gently lifted Ali's chin until she was looking into his eyes. "Are you getting this?"

"I didn't chase her. I didn't chase any of them. What did she say about my friends? Did she say she liked you?" Ali really didn't want to be having this discussion. She never should have agreed to this crazy ass idea.

"Unimportant."

"I thought you said it was important what they thought of my friends."

"No. That's what she said. She answered the question with one word—unimportant."

"Oh."

"Ali, are you seeing a pattern here, or not?"

"We've only gotten two responses so far, how can there be a pattern?" She drained the last of her fourth margarita.

"What did you like about Janet?"

Ali rolled her eyes. "She was very pretty, nice—um—nice and pretty."

"Did you feel a connection to her?"

A connection? Ali hadn't even thought about having a connection—with her—or—wait. Wait a minute. Was that the pattern? She'd had a series of relationships with the women on that list, but did she feel a connection to any of them? Yes, she had had a connection with Madison. But apparently Madison hadn't felt the same. Their whole relationship had been one big fat lie. Forming real connections was hard after that. Maybe she never really tried to find a connection. Although according to Janet, she tried too hard at everything else.

"Ali?"

"Huh?" Ali mumbled, still lost in her thoughts.

"Connection?"

"I'm tired." She needed time to think about this. Time without Charley staring into her face waiting for an answer. "And more than a little drunk. Can we call it a night and pick this back up tomorrow?"

"I'm just trying to help you, Ali."

Ali stood and gave him a tight hug. "I know, and I love you for it. But my head is spinning, and I need to lie down, because the room is spinning faster than my head is. Make yourself comfortable in the guest room. You know where everything is."

Ali had just laid her head on her pillow when there was a knock on her bedroom door. "Who is it?" She laughed as if it was the funniest thing she ever heard.

Charley popped his head in. "Can I come in?" He didn't wait for an answer before opening the door fully and stepping in. He set a full glass of water on the nightstand. "Darling, you need to drink this before you go to sleep. All of it."

"Yes, Mother." She laughed again.

"How's your head?" He sat on the edge of the bed.

"I don't know. It's been flying around the room and I haven't been able to catch it."

"That good, huh?"

Ali sat up and grabbed the glass. "I definitely drank too much. How come your head is still attached to your body? You had as much to drink as I did."

"Baby, I've easily got an extra hundred pounds on you. Besides, I've been drinking since I was a toddler. You've only been drinking since you were a teen."

"Liar. You told me you didn't have your first drink until college."

"Just trying to see if you're paying attention." He stood. "Now drink that water and get some sleep. We'll check in the morning to see if anyone else answers your message."

Ali had almost forgotten that they were in the middle of untangling the truth about her love life. Almost. She knew she had a lot to think about, but she didn't have the strength to do it tonight. She needed her wits about her for that. She finished her water and fell into a fitful sleep. Her ex-girlfriends paraded through her dreams shouting out their opinions of her. When she ran out of exes, various celebrities joined the parade. Jennifer Aniston was particularly harsh. When Madison Parker entered the picture Ali sprang up, fully awake. What the hell had she just done?

CHAPTER TWO

Madison Parker set a cup of coffee in front of her sister. Jenny liked to get to the donut shop before it opened to go over any business they needed to take care of for the day. Madison would have preferred meeting at the end of the workday but gave in to her older sister's wishes. They had grown up in the donut shop, helping their dad after school and on weekends. When their father died five years ago, they took over, with Madison running the day-to-day operations and Jenny handling the financial and clerical side of things.

Jenny sported a new, shorter haircut that swung freely just above her shoulders. Madison liked it and wondered how she would look if she ever decided to cut her own long hair.

Francis had been in the back for the last two hours making the donuts for the day. Marco Parker, Madison and Jenny's father, had hired him more than eighteen years ago. The shop had been called Marco's Donut Shop then, but a freak lightning strike damaged the sign breaking off the first four letters. It wasn't long before everyone in town started referring to it as O's Donut Shop. When their father got around to getting the sign fixed, he adopted the new name and O's Donuts became official. Madison added cream and two packets of sugar to her coffee and glanced at her watch. The move didn't go unnoticed by Jenny.

"Somewhere you need to be? Hot date maybe?" It was a running joke that Madison was getting tired of. She hadn't had a hot date, or any date for that matter, for going on two years. She just didn't have the interest. Her last relationship left her hurting more than she cared to admit. Hurt seemed to be a running theme in her love life.

The truth was she was hoping to get a quick run in before the shop opened. It always helped clear her head. And if there was anything she needed today it was a clear head. They were hiring two new employees and she hated the interview and decision-making process. They had been shorthanded for the last couple of weeks, and Madison was getting sick of working the extra hours.

"Ha." She shook her head. "No. I'm done with dating and done with women for that matter. Don't need the drama." Or the heartache.

"Maddy, don't be like that. Just because your last relationship didn't work out doesn't mean there isn't some fantastic woman out there just waiting to meet you."

Madison ignored the comment. Jenny sorted through the pile of papers and mail on the table in front of her. She pulled out several sheets. "The electric bills from the past two months have gone up. It doesn't appear to be an increase in business. I'm thinking the oven is pulling more power than it used to. It is almost twenty years old after all. Maybe we should look into the cost of a new one." She paused, shuffled through the papers again, and retrieved an envelope. "Oh, and this came for you yesterday. No return address." She handed the envelope to Madison.

The postmark was too smudged to read, and she didn't recognize the handwriting. Probably just junk mail, disguised as a personal letter. She pushed it aside.

"Aren't you going to open it?"

"No. How much did the electric bill go up?" She was never going to have time for that run if they didn't get on with this.

They discussed the pro and cons of a new oven—decided against it for now—and what they were looking for in a new employee. Jenny wouldn't be available for the interviews today, and Madison assured her she could handle it on her own. They wrapped up with only ten minutes to spare before it was time to open. No run before work today.

Jenny gathered her papers, slipped them into a folder, and grabbed a fresh donut from the rack before heading out the door. Madison rarely indulged in their wares, preferring salads and vegetables to sweets. She sometimes envied Jenny's carefree ways.

"Hey, boss." Valerie had come in through the back door for her morning shift. She grabbed her apron from the hook on the wall and tied it around her waist. Her bleached blond hair was pulled neatly into a ponytail, giving her an even more youthful look than her twenty-something years. She had been with O's for over two years, and Madison knew they'd found a gem when they had hired her.

Madison slipped the envelope with no return address into her back pocket, greeted Valerie, and turned the sign on the door to OPEN. Several regulars made their way in. Some sat at tables, and a few made themselves comfortable at the counter. Madison set two coffee cups in front of a couple of elderly gentlemen at the counter and poured them each a cup of coffee. "How are you doing today, Joe? Tom?"

They graced the donut shop with their presence almost every morning. Madison loved listening to their stories and advice. She envied their obviously close relationship. They'd been together for over forty years, having to hide it from the world much of that time.

"Can't complain," Joe said. "No one wants to hear it anyway."

"Oh, honey, you can always complain to me." Tom gave him a kiss on the cheek. "Not that I want to hear it either." His bald head was in total contrast to his partner's thick gray hair.

Madison couldn't help but laugh. "You two are the best. What can I get for you?"

They placed their orders and made idle chitchat while they waited. The next several hours went pretty much the same as every other day, except for the job interviews. Madison narrowed the seven candidates down to two. Lea said she could start anytime—yes, Saturday would be fine—and Ellie could the following Monday. Madison ordered new name tags for them and readied the paperwork they would need to fill out when they started. She sent a text to Jenny to let her know the details.

Her phone rang before she had a chance to leave her office. It was Jenny. Probably had questions about the new employees, she reasoned.

"Did you have questions about who I hired?" Madison asked without saying hello.

"No, that's not why I'm calling."

"Everything okay with Patty and Grayson?" Patty was Jenny's daughter, and Grayson was Patty's two-year-old son. Not having kids of her own, Madison was very close to them. Jenny was on babysitting duty most weekdays.

"Everything's fine. I was just curious about that letter you got. Who's it from? Who writes actual letters these days?"

"What? You called me because of that?" Madison shook her head. Ridiculous.

"Yeah. Call me crazy, but for some reason it just seems strange to me," Jenny continued.

"You're crazy."

"Thanks."

"Don't tell me to do stuff if you don't really mean it." Madison had forgotten all about the letter.

"Well?"

"Hold on." She pulled the envelope from her pocket, ripped open one edge, and shook out the piece of paper inside. It was obviously printed from a computer. She glanced at the name printed on the bottom. Her stomach lurched and her breakfast threatened to come back up. The phone she'd been cradling between her head and shoulder slipped out and fell hard onto the desk, making her jump. She momentarily forgot about Jenny.

It was from Ali. Ali Daniels who had broken her heart twenty years ago. Ali Daniels who had disappeared from her life without a single word of explanation. What the hell?

Madison heard her name being called as if from another dimension, like she was having an out-of-body experience. It took her a few moments to realize that it was Jenny calling her name, still on the phone. "Sorry," Madison said into the mouthpiece.

"What just happened?"

"Um, well…"

"Madison? Are you all right?"

"Yeah. The letter is from Ali."

"Ali who? Ali your best friend from high school? That Ali?"

"Oh yeah. That Ali." Madison hesitated. No need to keep it a secret anymore. She was out now. Jenny knew she was gay. She'd just never bothered to tell her that Ali had been her first love. Her first lover. "Jen, she was so much more than my best friend."

"What do you mean?"

"I was in love with her."

There were several moments of silence. Madison assumed Jenny was letting that information sink in.

"Oh. Did she know?"

Madison took a step back in time, to the last time she saw Ali and the argument they had. She had just turned eighteen. She thought Ali had gotten over it. They had even talked after that. Then Ali was gone. Madison had reached out multiple times after that, but Ali wouldn't talk to her or see her. She finally gave up, her heart so heavy with pain she could barely manage to carry it around. "Yes. I thought she felt the same. We were together the last two years of high school. Secretly, of course. I thought we would be together forever."

"What happened? I remember you being sad and withdrawn right after you graduated. I thought maybe it had something to do with you coming out and being sad because you were alone."

"I was devastated because of Ali. She just disappeared out of my life without a word." Her hurt had turned to anger over the years. The tightness in her chest told her she had never let go of that rage.

"Why?"

Madison shook her head, even though Jenny couldn't see her. "Damned if I know. Hard to get answers from someone who won't talk to you."

"What does the letter say?"

Madison realized she hadn't read anything but Ali's name. She wasn't sure she wanted to read the rest.

"Madison?"

"I don't know."

"Read it. Out loud."

Madison cleared her throat and began to read. "*Hi,*" Madison paused. "Oh my God, she didn't even use my name. This looks like some sort of form letter."

"Just read it," Jenny told her.

She continued. "*I know we haven't spoken in a while. I hope you are doing well. I am working on self-improvement, trying to become a better person and thus a better partner in a relationship. I'm hoping you can help me out by answering some questions for me. I would really appreciate it. Yours truly, Ali (your ex).*" Your ex? As if Ali had to explain who she was. As if Madison had forgotten her. Could ever forget her. She certainly had tried.

Jenny interrupted her thoughts. "That's awful ballsy. She wants you to help her in a relationship with someone else?"

"Apparently." Pretty shitty thing to ask someone. She wadded up the piece of paper and threw it across the office, just missing the trash can. "Fuck. And fuck her. I'm not answering her stupid questions. She can just go screw herself."

"Tell me how you really feel?"

Madison knew Jenny was trying to make light of the situation, trying to help calm Madison down. It wasn't helping.

"Who the hell does she think she is?" Madison asked.

"I'm sorry, Maddy, this has apparently opened an old wound."

It had for sure. A wound that Madison thought had long since healed over. A wound that was twenty years old. How could it possibly be affecting her this much now?

"Why don't you take the rest of the day off? Go for a run. Clear your head."

Madison glanced at her watch. "I can't. We're shorthanded. Remember?"

"Oh yeah. I'm sorry I can't help."

"That's okay. I'll manage." She would just have to push this crap from her head and get herself back into business mode. She needed to get back out on the floor before Valerie got overwhelmed.

"Tell you what, Patty should be home from work by four. I'll come in then and relieve you."

"I got this. I'm not going to let an asshole ghost from my past ruin my day." But she already felt like it was ruined. Damn her. Ali Daniels. What the hell could she have been thinking sending something like that to her?

CHAPTER THREE

Ali was surprised that every single ex had answered her—everyone except Madison. The common theme she was seeing—okay, Charley pointed it out—was that no one felt like Ali had been fully committed to the relationship or to them. It wasn't that she ever cheated. She just never had both feet in. She couldn't argue with that assessment. It had been almost two weeks since Charley had rushed out to the mail drop and deposited the letter to Madison. Ali didn't expect an answer from her. Of course, Ali had never expected Madison to do what she had done so many years ago, either. Ali chalked it up to one more slap in the face. Maybe she should thank Madison for the pain she had caused. That pain translated so easily into Ali's writing. Even now, Ali could draw on that pain to add authentic emotions to the characters in her books. It was easier for her to write pain than it was to write joy. She wrote nearly every day. It didn't matter if times were good or if they were bad. It didn't matter if she felt happy—maybe content was more accurate—or if her heart was breaking. Her writing was like a letter. Sometimes it was a love letter she wrote to no one. Sometimes it was a scream put down on paper so it wouldn't come bubbling out of her mouth or explode from her chest. She found the best words could be rung out of human suffering. After all, what didn't kill us, made us stronger. Of course, there was always the chance that it would kill us. But the hurt hadn't killed Ali so far. If it did anything it made her numb. She had put a shield around her emotions—a thick piece of bulletproof glass that no one had really been able to penetrate. She pondered what her life might have been like if she had never met Madison, or at least if she had never let her into her heart, never trusted her to keep it safe. She wondered if suffering was a necessary part of the human condition. What would people who never suffered be like? They would be happy, Ali reasoned. It was impossible to be truly happy inside the protective box she had built around herself. Sometimes she thought she could see the possibility of happiness, but when she reached for it, the most she could do was skim it with her fingertips.

The knock on her office door brought Ali out of her thoughts, startling her. Charley opened the door and stuck his head in.

"Working?" he asked.

"Remind me to keep my apartment locked," Ali said, only half kidding.

Charley let himself into the room. He hiked up the back of the flowered skirt he was wearing and plopped down on the easy chair in the corner. "You did," he said, holding up a set of keys. "I let myself in. Don't give me keys if you don't want me to use them, sweetie. Whatcha doing?"

Ali saved the three paragraphs she had managed to write on her laptop before thoughts of Madison had hijacked her brain. "My next book. It's been slow going."

"Still no word from Madison Parker?" Charley asked.

"Get out of my head."

"But I like it in there. It's so warm and cozy and has the best echo when I yell my name."

Ali shut her computer and turned her office chair to face Charley. "We don't need her input. We got enough info from the other responses."

Charley leaned forward. "And what did we learn?"

They'd gone over this already. Ali didn't feel like rehashing it. She shook her head.

"Ali, my dear, I'm just trying to help."

"I know and I love you for it. It just tires me out."

Charley pressed on. "Let's try to figure out why you never really felt connected to any of the women you dated." He paused. "With the obvious exception of Madison Parker." Ali hated the way he always referred to her by her first and last name. It made her seem somehow more formal. More important. But she *had* been important. That was the kicker. Extremely important.

"I really don't have an answer for that."

Charley put his hands out, indicating he wanted Ali to put her hands in his. She knew the routine and scooted her chair forward and placed her hands in his much larger ones. Charley looked into her eyes. "I think you need to go see Madison Parker."

Ali pulled her hands back with so much force her chair moved. "What? No way. Why would you even say that? No." She kicked off with her feet, sending her and her chair back to her desk.

"Me thinks you protest too much."

"Me thinks you are out of your mind. Why would I want to do that?"

"Because whatever happened between the two of you has somehow stymied your ability to have a meaningful relationship."

"I'm not disagreeing with you. She hurt me bad. But why do I need to see her to figure it out?"

"Because you obviously haven't been able to do it on your own."

Ali still wasn't convinced. The thought of seeing Madison again was both terrifying—and even though she hated to admit it—exhilarating. "No way," she said with more force than she meant to.

"Oh, baby, what? Talk to me. Why does it make you so angry? Or is it fear?" Charley's voice softened.

Ali let out an exasperated huff. "Damned if I know."

"You seem to have so many emotions tied up in this woman that you don't have any left over for anyone else. If nothing else, baby, you need closure, even if she refuses to give you any answers."

Charley's words were like a hammer slamming into the fragile wall that she had built around her emotions, and the truth of them struck her like a fist. Without her realizing it she had given Madison control over her. It was damn well time to get it back. If Madison didn't have answers for her, at least she would be able to give Madison a piece of her mind. Let her know just how much she had hurt her.

"I hope I don't live to regret this, but I'm going to admit that you may be right. I think I need to take a trip to my old hometown and talk to Madison face-to-face." Even as she was saying the words, Ali was afraid she might be making the biggest mistake of her life.

CHAPTER FOUR

The trip to Maryland left Ali with plenty of time to think. Too much time. She almost turned around and went home no less than five times. Charley volunteered to go along on the trip, of course, but Ali decided she needed to do this alone. Besides, Charley was only a phone call away if Ali needed him. The five-and-a-half-hour trip felt more like five and a half days. She hadn't been back to Clyde since her parents moved to Florida shortly after Ali left for college. It was a weird feeling heading back there. It certainly wasn't home anymore, although it apparently still held a piece of her heart, or rather Madison did, and Ali was determined to get it back.

Ali thought back to the last time she saw Madison. It sent a surge of acid into her stomach that worked its way up her throat. She did her best to swallow it back down without much luck. She remembered it like it was yesterday.

She'd just gotten home from her summer job. Her mother handed her a note Madison had left for her.

It sounded innocent enough. *I have something important to tell you. Can you come over when you get home? This news needs to be told face to face.*

Ali jumped on her bike and rode the two blocks to Madison's house. She went around to the back of the house, silently slipped through the gate, and stopped dead in her tracks. There was Madison. Madison, the woman she loved. Madison, the person she thought she'd spend the rest of her life with—kissing Howard Dallas. Kissing. Howard. Dallas.

No wonder Madison had refused to come out to her parents. Had refused to tell her father no when he insisted that Madison go to the prom with Howard, the son of his best friend. Madison hadn't been in love with her at all. She was in love with Howard Dallas. It had been so obvious in that moment. So life shattering. So soul crushing. No wonder Ali had such a hard time finding a real relationship. Madison had sucked her heart out and shredded it. Shredded it with Howard Dallas. She had slipped out as silently as she had slipped in. She didn't need to hear what Madison wanted to tell her. She had just witnessed it. Hearing it would only make it more real. More devastating. So many of Ali's decisions in life were based on that moment, now frozen in time. She deleted her email address, eliminating the possibility of Madison contacting her through Instant Messenger, and went to Syracuse University for the summer semester instead of waiting till the fall. She not only needed to get away from Madison, she needed to get away from the very town she lived in. It was a great relief when her parents moved to Florida, eliminating any need for Ali to ever return to Clyde.

Ali jumped when her phone rang. She pressed the button on her steering wheel answering the call through her car. "Hi, Charley."

"Hi, baby doll. How are you doing?"

"Fine. If fine means I feel like throwing up."

"You got this, darling. I have total faith in you."

"That makes one of us."

They chatted for almost an hour. It helped quite a bit to calm Ali's nerves. What did you say to someone you hadn't seen since high school? It wasn't like she could walk into O's—whatever that was—*and say hey, girl, what's up?* She and Charley had discussed it, and of course Charley had suggestions, but Ali still didn't really have a plan. They were still talking when Ali got off the exit to her old hometown. It felt familiar, yet strangely alien. She followed her GPS directions to O's and was surprised when she parked across the street and realized it was the donut shop Madison's father used to own. Ali wondered if it had changed hands or simply changed names. She had spent many weekends in that shop hanging out with Madison, sometimes lending a hand when things got busy.

She parked across the street from the shop, between a pickup truck with a gun rack in the back window and a small car with the bumper held on with duct tape. Typical small-town life, Ali thought sarcastically. Thank God, I don't live here anymore.

"Charley, tell me I can do this," she said.

"You can do this. Take several deep breaths, get out of the car, and walk in like you own the place. Be nice but be firm."

"Maybe I should go to the hotel first and come back here in the morning." Ali leaned her head back and closed her eyes. She opened them in time to see someone running past on the opposite side of the quiet street. It took her several seconds to realize it was Madison. Ali slid down in her seat but watched Madison in the rearview mirror. Shit.

The warm May air felt good in Madison's lungs as her feet pounded the pavement. She turned right, leaving the paved street, and continued to the trail that would take her around Miller's Pond, her favorite place to run. Bits of gravel crunched under her feet and birds chirped above her as they danced about in the trees. She increased her pace, letting her movement become her meditation. She knew at this pace it would take her about twenty minutes to make it all the way around the pond. She waved as she passed a couple of elderly gentlemen fishing. They waved back with a smile. This was why she loved this small town. Everyone was so friendly, whether they knew you or not. She could never understand why anyone would want to live in a city where no one knew their neighbors. This place had heart. It had a big piece of *her* heart.

Madison slowed her stride as she came to the end of the trail at the same spot she had entered it. Back on the street, she jogged in place for a bit to let her muscles cool down slowly before entering the back door of the donut shop. A quick check-in with Valerie and her new employee, Lea, told her all was going well. Lea was working out great. She hoped Ellie would as well. She grabbed a bottle of cold water from the fridge and her car keys from her office and headed to her car in the back parking lot. She ignored the twinge in her back as she slid into the seat. It had given her trouble from time to time, and even gone out once, putting her out of commission for a few days, but she refused to give in to it now.

After a hot shower to help relax her back and a fresh change of clothes at home, Madison walked the block and a half to her sister's house for dinner. The smell of pot roast greeted her as she let herself in. She walked through the living room that was impeccably decorated and spotless except for a few random toddler toys piled haphazardly in the corner, remnants of Jenny babysitting her grandson, Grayson.

"Hey there," Jenny said as Madison entered the kitchen, which was almost as spotless even though Jenny was in the midst of making supper. "You're just in time to mash the potatoes for me."

"I thought that was Jimmy's job." Jenny had the kind of marriage Madison had always hoped to find but couldn't seem to even get close to.

"He has to work late. He said not to wait for him."

Madison found the masher in the drawer, added a little butter and milk to the pan with the potatoes, and set to work.

"How ya doing?" Jenny asked.

"Fine."

Jenny stopped tossing the salad and turned her full attention to her. "How are you really doing? You've seemed a little off since you got that letter from Ali."

Madison scooped a bit of mashed potatoes from the pan with her finger and stuck it in her mouth. It gave her a moment to think and formulate her answer. "I guess it did throw me. I never expected to hear from her again after all these years. And it was really shitty the way she did it."

Jenny sat at the table and patted the seat next to her. "Sit. Let's talk."

Madison sat, silently waiting for Jenny to start. She wasn't about to volunteer any information; she wanted to forget the whole letter thing and even more so Ali. If Jenny wanted to know anything she would have to ask.

"Want to tell me what happened with Ali that seems to still have you in knots twenty years later?"

"Just because she pissed me off with that letter doesn't mean I'm in knots over her. I got over her a long time ago." She wasn't sure if she was trying to convince Jenny or herself. How could someone who was a part of her life so long ago have any hold on her now? Granted she was the most important person in her life back then, but they were kids. It obviously didn't mean as much to Ali as it had meant to her, so why give her any power now?

"Okay. Whatever you say. But tell me what happened back then. If memory serves, I would have been returning from my junior year in college when you two broke up."

Madison let out a huff. "There was no breakup. She just left. No good-bye. No note. No nothing." She realized she said the last part a little more harshly than she intended.

"But why?"

"Why what? Why did she leave without a word?"

Jenny nodded.

"I don't know. We had had a bit of an argument over me going to the prom with Howard. But I thought we were okay."

"Why did you go to the prom with him if you were with Ali?"

"Believe me it wasn't my idea. Dad wanted me to go with him. He didn't know about my relationship with Ali, and at that point I didn't feel like I could tell him. Or anyone for that matter."

"So, you went to the prom with Howard and then Ali disappeared?"

Madison took a deep breath. She hadn't thought about this for years but had replayed it in her mind at least a dozen times since Ali's letter had arrived. "Not exactly. I went to the prom with Howard, like Dad wanted. Ali went stag and I spent most of the time talking to her. She wanted to come out and asked me to do the same. I didn't think I was ready. I thought she understood. We ended the night on a good note. I thought about what she wanted, and I did tell Mom and Dad that I'm gay the day after the prom."

"I remember that. I remember you called me at college and told me. It was probably a few days later. But you didn't tell me you were with Ali."

"That's because when I told you, Ali was already gone. And I hadn't told Mom and Dad about being with Ali because I thought she should have the chance to tell her parents first."

"What changed between the prom and her suddenly leaving?"

"That's what I don't know. After I told Mom and Dad, I went to Ali's house to tell her I'd come out to them. She wasn't home, so I left a note with her mom asking her to come over. I wanted to tell her in person. She never showed and I never heard from her again."

"And you tried to reach her?"

Madison had tried every way she could think of to get in touch with her. She tried for months. "Yes. Of course. I called. I emailed. I went to her house. Her mother always said she wasn't home. I'm not sure if she was lying or if Ali had already left town. I had no choice but to give up. Believe me, it wasn't easy," Madison said.

"No wonder you were so upset when her letter showed up out of nowhere."

"I really don't know why she left my life without a word. And I don't know why she would send me a letter like that out of nowhere. Why in the world would she ever expect me to help her after what she did?" She shook her head. She was tired of this conversation. They could talk it to death and still not have answers. She got up, opened a couple of cabinets and found a large bowl.

"Do you think maybe you should write her back?" Jenny continued.

Madison scooped a large spoonful of mashed potatoes into the bowl, keenly aware of her desire to throw the whole pan across the room. She was not only angry at Ali—she was angry at Ali's ability to affect her emotions so much after all these years. "And why would I want to do that?" Her back was to Jenny and she made no attempt to turn around. She could feel the heat in her face rising.

"To let her know how much she hurt you."

Madison turned to look at her sister. "And what good would that do? There is no way in hell she could leave me like that and not know how much it was going to hurt. It didn't make sense to me then and this doesn't make sense to me now."

"Then maybe write back and ask her why she left the way she did."

Madison finished with the potatoes and grabbed a wine glass from the shelf above the sink. She had to stand on her tiptoes to reach it. Jenny was a good three inches taller than her and seemed to keep everything higher than Madison would have preferred it. "There's an open bottle of red on the dining room table," Jenny said without being asked. Madison retrieved the bottle and poured herself a glass. She held the bottle up, silently asking Jenny if she wanted some. Jenny shook her head. Several beats of silence went by.

"So?" Jenny asked.

"What?"

"So, do you think you should write and ask why she left?"

"No."

"Why not?"

Madison took a long sip of her wine and let the warmth of it settle in her stomach. "Because I don't care anymore. She had her chance. Hell, she had twenty years. I refuse to open that door again. She's just not worth it."

"But—"

Madison held up her hand. She did something she almost never did. She shut her sister down. "I'm done talking about it. She is out of my life and has been for a long time." Out of her life? Yes. Out of her head? Maybe not so much. Out of her heart? That was something she didn't want to think about.

Jenny got up and turned the oven off. She gathered up plates and silverware and set them on the counter. "Maddy, you really do need to—"

"Stop, Jen. Stop." She needed Jenny to stop talking about it and she needed to get any thoughts of Ali out of her head. She wasn't sure she could do the latter.

CHAPTER FIVE

Ali hadn't expected the visceral response from her body at the sight of Madison. She hadn't gotten a good look, but she knew without a doubt when she ran by who it was. The pounding in her chest made its way to her head and she thought the sound might explode from her ears. She sucked in her breath so fast that she choked on her own spit. The girl she had loved so deeply was now a full-grown woman. Somehow in her head Madison had remained that eighteen-year-old girl who broke her heart.

She had watched Madison in her rearview mirror until Madison was out of sight. She wasn't sure what to do next. Wait for her to return? Go in the donut shop and ask questions about Madison? No. Neither of those options felt right. She needed to better prepare herself for this. This? What was this? This was a mistake. What could she possibly learn about relationships from the one person who had fucked up their relationship so badly that Ali had left her hometown never to return—until now? She had the urge to call Charley, but she knew exactly what Charley would tell her. *You need to stay the course, baby doll. You're there now. Follow through. Learn what you can, and if there is nothing to learn, tell her the fuck off.*

"Okay. Okay. Get out of my head, Charley," she said out loud. She'd booked a room at one of the two motels in town. She briefly considered stopping at a fast-food joint to get something to eat as she drove to the Sleep Well Motel, but her stomach objected, and she relented. She didn't know if Grubhub was available in this sleepy town if she got hungry later, and she really didn't care enough to check the app on her phone.

The motel room was nicer than Ali expected, although it did look like it had about eight coats of paint on the woodwork. She flipped on the television, but nothing on the screen registered as her brain played out every scenario possible when she did walk into that donut shop to confront Madison. She was getting herself ready for bed when her phone rang out Charley's ring tone. She knew Charley was waiting for an update. "Hey," Ali said.

"Honey child, I have been waiting for you to call me. Have you been with Madison Parker all this time?"

Ali slipped her pajama bottoms on with one hand while holding the phone with the other. Not the easiest thing to do. "No. I didn't go in."

"Say what? Why not?"

"I'm just not ready. I'll go in the morning. I did, however, see Madison." Ali explained the brief sighting.

"You didn't try to talk to her?"

Ali turned the thermostat up on the heater lining the wall under the large window. She hadn't noticed how chilly the room was when she first arrived. "What was I supposed to do, chase her down?"

"Good point." They chatted for several more minutes, with most of that time spent with Charley making sure Ali wasn't changing her mind. "You know this is important, right?"

Ali hated to admit it, but she knew Charley was right. She had to find closure with Madison one way or another or she would never be able to have a decent relationship. "Yes."

"Okay, sweetie, get some sleep. Call me tomorrow."

But sleep wasn't Ali's friend that night. She tossed and turned and tossed some more. She finally fell into a deep sleep just as the sun was coming up. It was nine o'clock when she opened her eyes. She'd gotten a solid three hours of rest. A hot shower helped to dislodge the grogginess from her eyes and brain.

"Time to make the donuts," she singsonged to herself on her way to O's. The silly jingle somehow helped to calm her nerves. She had no idea if Madison would be working or how she would react if she was there. She parked in the same spot she had the day before and sat in her car for a full ten minutes before extracting herself and walking across the street. A tingle ran up her arm as she touched the door handle on the donut shop. Fear? Anxiety? Excitement at seeing Madison again? All of the above. She took a deep breath and pushed the door open. The smell of warm donuts was both comforting and disturbing. The place had been updated with new booths and a shiny new counter, but still held the same charm it always did. It looked bigger than she remembered, and she realized they must have expanded into what used to be a pizza shop next door.

She spotted Madison right away, pouring coffee into the cup of an elderly man seated at the counter. There were fine laugh lines around her eyes and a couple of lines etched on either side of her mouth. A few stray pieces of gray hair mixed with her dark brown hair at the temples. She still wore it long. She looked older but was just as beautiful as Ali remembered. Her brown eyes still held the same sparkle, framed by gorgeous thick lashes.

Ali's heart moved up to her throat, and she found it hard to breathe. She was transported back to high school, to secretly meeting for coordinated bathroom breaks for a quick kiss, to sleepovers where very little actual sleeping was done, to making love in Madison's bed, to…

Madison looked up and caught her eye. Ali didn't know anyone could open their eyes or their mouth that wide. The look of shock on Madison's face would have been comical if Ali hadn't had her heart drop from her throat to the pit of her stomach. She suddenly felt like she might throw up and didn't know whether to leave or run to the restroom.

"Feel free to sit anywhere there's an open seat," a voice to her right said.

Ali jumped.

It was a waitress, Lea, according to her name tag. "And welcome to O's," she said.

"Huh? Um. Yeah. Okay. Um." Ali realized she wasn't making any sense. She started for a booth, changed her mind, and turned in the direction of the counter and Madison, changed her mind again, and slipped into a booth off to the side. Once she was seated, she wasn't sure she had made the right decision coming here. Lea was standing over her with her order pad in hand.

"Can I get you a cup of coffee or tea to start?" Lea laid a menu in front of her.

Ali looked over at Madison, who was still staring at her. "Coffee—and—and could you please ask Madison to come over here for a few minutes? Please. Thanks. Please," Ali mumbled. Shit. She was rambling. She must have sounded like an idiot.

"Sure thing," Lea replied.

Ali watched Lea approach Madison, exchange a few words with her, nodding in Ali's direction, and disappear into the back. Madison continued to stare at her, and just when Ali was sure she would disappear into the back like Lea had—or even into thin air—she headed in Ali's direction, coffee pot in hand.

Madison flipped the coffee cup that was on Ali's table right side up and poured coffee into it. "What can I get for you?"

Ali was confused. Surely, she had recognized her. The look on her face told Ali as much. Why was she acting like this? Was she that much of a bitch? It wasn't enough that she had thrown Ali away and chosen Howard? Now she had to pretend Ali was just another customer. "Madison," she started. "Madison." She wasn't sure what to say. Madison didn't respond.

"Madison," Ali repeated. "Can we talk?"

"I'm thinking no. You could have talked to me twenty years ago, but you decided not to. That's on you. Not me. I am in no mood to talk to you now."

Ali hadn't known what to expect, but this wasn't it. "Why?" It was the only thing she could think to say.

"There's no point. Now would you like to order?"

"You broke my heart. I think I deserve a few minutes of your time."

Madison put her hand on her hip and dipped her chin down. "Excuse me? What the hell are you talking about?" A few of the customers in the shop turned toward them. Madison lowered her voice. "You come into my place of business and demand to talk to me with some bullshit accusations? You have some nerve."

The nauseous feeling Ali had when she saw Madison was quickly being replaced by anger. She had driven a long way to talk to Madison and Madison was acting like an ass. Madison should have been begging for forgiveness, not treating Ali like she was in the wrong.

"Madison, I have no idea what *you* are so mad about. I just want to talk. I'm the one who has every right to be angry." Ali worked to keep her voice steady. She knew that agitating Madison would only make matters worse.

"No." Madison turned and walked away.

Ali watched in silence as Madison left her—once more. She clenched her jaw so hard she gave herself an instant headache. She took a large gulp of her coffee, hoping the caffeine would help. The fact that it was steaming hot and burned her tongue was no help at all.

Charley. She needed to talk to Charley. Ali typed out a text.

Ali: *I'm at O's and saw Madison, but she refuses to talk to me.*

Charley: *Oh baby. What are you going to do?*

Ali: *I'm more determined than ever to get answers from her. She actually said my accusation—her word—that she broke my heart was bullshit.*

Charley: *What? I am confused. Of course she broke your heart.*

Ali: *I'm confused too. She seems to be making shit up in her head. I think I'm going to sit here, all day if necessary, until she decides to talk to me. I'll just order donuts all day.*

Charley: *Donuts?*

Ali: *Oh yeah. O's is a donut shop.*

Charley: *Stupid name.*

Ali: *This whole thing is stupid.*

Charley: *Good luck, baby. You got this.*

Ali: *Thanks. I'll call you later.*

Lea reappeared. "Have you decided?" Ali ordered a half dozen assorted donuts. She added four small containers of flavored creamer to her coffee and took another tentative sip. A plethora of emotions coursed through her. Anger. Confusion. Determination. Attraction. Wait. What? Attraction? After everything Madison had done to her, she was still attracted to her? That just didn't make sense. None of this made sense. Why was she even here?

But she knew the answer to that. She was here because she needed answers. And she was determined to get them. No matter how long it took.

CHAPTER SIX

I'll be in my office for a few minutes," Madison said to Valerie. "You and Lea okay for a bit without me?"

"Of course. Everything all right?"

Madison just nodded. She closed the office door behind her, slumped into her chair, and clenched her fists. What the hell? What the actual hell? What did Ali think she was doing showing up here and demanding to talk to her?

Madison let out a growl through clenched teeth and slammed her fist on the desk, sending a cup of pens and pencils flying. "You okay in there, boss?" Francis said, standing in the doorway.

"Yep. Just dropped something. I'm fine," Madison answered. But she was far from fine. She was furious. Ali didn't want to talk to her after high school, Madison certainly wasn't going to give her that chance now. When Ali cut off all communication, Madison had been devastated. Devastated! The only feeling she had for Ali now was hate. She knew she needed to work on letting that go. The only person hate would hurt was herself. But for now, she wanted to cling to that feeling. It was the only thing that felt real. It was like she was living in the twilight zone.

"I hurt her?" she whispered. "How the hell does she figure that?"

You have fun rewriting history, Ali. Your history belongs to you—have at it. My history belongs to me and I choose to keep mine honest even with all the pain. So, fuck you. I stopped waiting for you a long time ago. That ship has sailed. I'm waiting for it to cross the horizon and be out of sight, once again. I am emptying my heart of you. Sail away.

Madison wondered how long Ali would stay in the donut shop before giving up and going back to whatever rock she had crawled out from under. She knew she couldn't stay in her office much longer. The breakfast crowd was winding down, but the lunch crowd would be revving up soon. They had expanded to serving soup, sandwiches, and pizza several years ago, greatly increasing business. She gave herself twenty minutes to get her anger under control and quietly slipped back behind the counter.

Ali was still there, quietly munching on donuts and looking at her phone. Madison gave herself permission to take in the woman her teenage lover had become. Her once long light brown hair now hung a few inches above her shoulders. No gray in sight. Madison suspected that was due to a good dye job. In fact, Ali's hair looked a shade or two lighter than it was in high school. Definitely dyed.

She couldn't count the number of times she had run her hands through that hair, feeling its silky texture and smelling faintly of vanilla scented shampoo. She rubbed her hands together trying to dislodge the memory. Ali had put on a few pounds, but the extra weight looked good on her. Up close, Madison had noticed the same deep blue eyes she'd remembered. She was still attractive. Madison found it infuriating.

The day seemed to drag on while customers came and went and still Ali sat there. Lea left at four o'clock, and when Ellie, the new girl, came in for her shift, Madison assigned her the booth Ali was in, even though she was technically still in training. Madison didn't plan on going near that table again. Madison's day didn't end until closing time at eight o'clock. Of course, Ali would show up on her one long day of the week.

Maybe she should just sit down and let Ali talk so she would leave. Madison wasn't sure if she could control her temper, which was usually pretty mild, if Ali said anything else stupid, which Madison was sure she would. She made up her mind to wait until the shop closed and if Ali was still there, she would give her a few minutes to state her case and then send her packing, hopefully never to be seen again.

Just as she had predicted, Ali was still sitting there, nine hours after she had arrived. She had determination. Madison would give her that. Valerie's shift had ended two hours ago. Only Ali, Ellie, and Madison remained.

Ali stretched her arms above her head. Her back was stiff, and her butt was sore, but it was closing time and Madison would have no choice but to talk to her now—or call the police to get her out.

She watched as the last customer walked out the door and Madison turned the sign in the window around to read CLOSED. Ellie hung up her apron and whispered something to Madison, nodding in Ali's direction. Madison must have told her it was okay to leave because she exited through the back.

Madison continued to stack menus, straighten chairs, and even sweep the floor, avoiding the booth Ali occupied. Ali half expected her to turn off the lights and leave with Ali still inside. She was surprised when Madison set the broom aside and slid into the booth across from her.

She sat there with her hands folded in front of her, staring at Ali but not saying a word. Now that she had Madison's full attention she didn't know where to start. There were so many things she wanted—needed—to know. Why had Madison chosen Howard over her? Was anything they had real? Was Madison straight? Bi? Had she ever meant anything to her?

"Why? Why wasn't I enough?" Ali said, surprising herself that that was her first question. She willed the tears that threatened to spill from her eyes to back off.

"You've got to be kidding me." Madison laughed sarcastically.

Ali couldn't believe her reaction. "Is this a joke to you? You broke my heart, Madison."

"And how exactly did I do that when you were the one who took off without even saying good-bye. You were the one who ignored my emails and phone calls. I tried to reach out to you in so many ways. So many times. Tell me exactly why you were the one with the broken heart?"

"Because you chose Howard over me. Don't act like that didn't happen." Her heart pounded in her chest and she found it hard to breathe.

"What?"

"I saw you, Madison. I saw you kissing him. I knew you were going to tell me it was over between us and I couldn't bear to hear you say the words."

"Ali, I have no idea what you're talking about."

So, they were going to play this game? Madison was going to deny everything. What good would that do now? The damage had already been done, a long time ago. Okay, she could play along—but once the truth was said out loud Madison would have no choice but to admit what she did and the effect it had on Ali.

"I came over to your house when I got your note. You said you had something important to tell me. I saw you and Howard in the backyard—kissing. I knew in that moment exactly what you wanted to tell me. I left before you had the chance, saving you the trouble and saving me the heartache from actually hearing you say it. That is why I disappeared from your life. That is why I couldn't bear to face you. The pain was just too great."

Madison seemed to think for a minute. Ali knew she had her. There was no denying it now. Ali watched as several different emotions scattered across Madison's face. She was quiet for several long beats with her hand over her mouth.

"Oh, is it all coming back to you now? Are you going to tell me that you had no idea how much that was going to hurt me?"

"Ali, you've got it all wrong."

"How could I have it wrong if I saw it with my own eyes? Huh? Tell me that." She realized she was raising her voice to match the level of frustration and anger that had crept in.

"How long did you watch us?"

"Watch you? Kissing? Why would I want to stay around and witness that? I saw you and I left."

"Ali, if you had stayed two seconds longer you would have seen me push Howard away. He kissed me without my consent, and I didn't want it. I wanted you. But you never showed up. At least I thought you didn't."

"What are you saying?" Confusion was edging out the feeling of anger.

"I'm saying Howard kissed me after I told him I'm gay. He came over and was getting way too—"

"You told him what?" Ali wasn't sure she had heard Madison correctly. Why would she tell Howard she was gay when she had refused to tell her parents?

"He asked me to go out with him and wouldn't take no for an answer. I told him I was gay, hoping the truth would make him back off. But he grabbed me and kissed me instead. I guess he thought he could change me. I don't know." She hesitated, seeming to gather her thoughts. "I never asked him his motives. I just pushed him away and told him to get the hell away from me. You must have seen him kiss me and got the wrong impression."

Wait. What? Madison wasn't willingly kissing him? She wasn't cheating? She wasn't going to choose him? Ali's stomach lurched. She left Madison because she had gotten the wrong impression. How was that even possible? This wasn't computing. "What are you trying to tell me?"

"Oh my God, Ali. You thought I was leaving you and you decided to leave me first. You never even gave me a chance to explain. How could you do that?"

Ali was at a loss for words. How could that have happened? She was so sure Madison was kissing Howard. True it was only for a second or two, but she couldn't stand the sight of them together. "But you said you had something to tell me. I thought you were going to tell me we were breaking up."

"I wanted to tell you in person that I had told my parents that I was gay. Ali, I thought you would be so happy. I wanted to see your face when I told you," Madison said, her voice shaking.

"I'm…" But Ali couldn't finish the sentence. The gravity of what she had done hit her in the chest causing a rush of tears. She lost Madison so long ago, not because of something Madison had done, but because of something she had done. How could she have been so stupid?

Just when she thought her tears were under control, they started all over again. Madison pulled a few napkins from the holder on the table and handed them to her. She didn't deserve even the smallest gesture of kindness from Madison. She deserved to have her tears stream down her face and ruin her shirt, seep into her heart, and drown her. She had made the biggest mistake of her life and had been paying for it ever since. Not only that but she had hurt the woman she loved and lost her as a result of her own stupidity.

She wiped her eyes and blew her nose. "Thanks," she managed to squeak out. "Madison, I'm so sorry. I didn't know."

"You didn't know because you never gave me a chance to explain. You didn't trust me." Madison's voice went up by a few decibels. "*You* are the one who broke *my* heart. Not the other way around. You have no one to blame for your suffering but yourself."

"I know that now."

"I think you should leave. I listened to what you had to say. We're done here." Madison stood up.

"No. Wait. Can't we talk about this? Figure out what to do now?" Ali's feelings rushed to the surface. She realized, much to her surprise, that she had never stopped loving Madison. She had to make this right. She had to make up for all the time they had lost out on because of her.

"Figure what out? You made your decision twenty years ago. There is nothing more to figure out. I've moved on with my life."

"You can't mean that. Is there someone else? I mean are you with someone?"

Madison didn't want to answer that. It was really none of Ali's business what she did with her life. "Let me tell you something I've learned, Ali. Life is made up of a series of decisions. Some of the choices we face are clear-cut right or wrong, while others have fuzzy lines and gray areas. There are times in our lives when we believe we are making the right decision but later second-guess ourselves. We have to ask ourselves if our intentions are pure. Or did we react too impulsively? Are there answers to these questions or is it all just a gray area? *Your* decisions brought us where we are today. Yours. You chose the gray areas. You made up your own answers."

"I don't understand," Ali said

"The goal of life is survival—followed by happiness. At what point does the need for happiness outweigh the commitments that have been made? Is the payout in the end worth the struggles of the journey? The payment for me has been a life without you. It took me years to recover my happiness. Do you hear me, Ali? Years. I am not willing to give up my happiness for a commitment we made to each other when we were eighteen. That commitment, by the way, was the one *you* threw away, not me. My happiness was gone and all I had left was survival mode." Madison paused to let her words sink in.

More tears escaped Ali's eyes. Madison refused to feel sorry for her. "I survived, although there were times I was sure I wouldn't. My life now is what I made it—without you. I don't need you in my life fucking it up. Go home, Ali." With that, Madison marched out of room and into her office, flipping off most of the lights on the way. She barely got the door closed when she burst into tears, so thankful she had been able to hold it together until she was away from Ali.

Well, now she knew why Ali had deserted her without a word. It didn't make her feel any better. In fact, she was even angrier now. Angry as hell. How could Ali have done that? She never even gave Madison a chance to explain. She just jumped to a conclusion and that was that. Obviously, their relationship had meant more to Madison than it had to Ali. Otherwise she wouldn't have thrown it all away so easily.

She pulled her phone from her pocket and attempted to pull up her contacts. Her vision was too blurry from tears to see clearly. Getting her emotions under control before she called Jenny was probably a better idea anyway. Her mother used to say *We get what we need, whether we like it or not.* "I guess I needed Ali out of my life, if this is the kind of person she is," she said to herself.

She had tried to hide the fact that Ali was her girlfriend, even after she told her parents she was gay. But her pain had been too great, and Ali's disappearance was obvious. She finally confessed the truth to her mother after much prompting. Her mother held her while she cried, on more than one occasion. She wished her mother was alive to hold her now. She shook her head. This was ridiculous. She had gotten over Ali years ago. She'd had a few relationships since then. Okay, none of them had lasted more than a few years, but that didn't diminish their importance. Ali showing up now didn't diminish them either. It didn't change anything.

Madison stayed in her office for over an hour. The crying barely lasted fifteen minutes before she got it under control. She cautiously stuck her head into the shop, half expecting to see Ali still sitting there, and fully prepared to call the police if she was. To her relief, the place was empty. She locked the door, shut off the rest of the lights, and went out the back door. She breathed an audible sigh as she made her way to her car in the deserted parking lot. A quick look at her phone told her it wasn't too late to call Jenny, but she decided that with her emotions now under control she could wait until their morning meeting to fill Jenny in. She felt stupid for her earlier reaction anyway. Not the anger, that was justified. She felt stupid for all the tears she shed over someone who didn't deserve a second thought, let alone tears.

She decided on her short drive home that she would just put Ali out of her head. There was no sense rehashing their conversation tonight, let alone what had happened so many years ago. But her brain had other ideas, and her mind returned again and again to Ali. The drink she made herself once she was home didn't do much to help. The more Ali appeared in her thoughts, the angrier Madison got. She had to figure out a way to get her out of her head. Only time had done that so many years ago, but she wasn't willing to give Ali or thoughts of her any more time. That door needed to be closed—and dead-bolted shut. Never to be opened again. That was the plan anyway.

CHAPTER SEVEN

Ali slipped the key card into the lock on her motel room door. Her head was swimming. Charley had called her on her drive back to the motel, but she hadn't answered it. She wasn't ready to talk about this. She needed to process it first. Images of Madison and Howard kissing ran through her brain and coursed through her veins making her feel sick to her stomach. This was nothing new. It had happened periodically, without her consent, throughout the years. What was new was what followed.

Madison said she'd pushed Howard away. Ali could see that happening now. She added that image to the old one, and everything changed. Madison wasn't cheating on her or breaking up with her. Ali was actually the one who did the breaking up. That fact weighed heavy on her now. She had broken Madison's heart, not the other way around.

Her phone rang again as she turned the shower on. Sitting in a donut shop all day left her feeling a little greasy and powdered sugary—if that was even a thing. She took a second to decide what to do and turned the water off. Landing heavily on the bed, she pressed the answer button on her phone.

"Honey child, you have left me hanging all day. What happened? Did you get answers or give Madison Parker a piece of your mind?" Charley didn't bother with pleasantries. That was something Ali usually liked about him. He got right to the meat of the matter.

"By the time we got done talking I didn't have much of my mind left to give her."

"Let's not talk in riddles here. Tell me."

Ali let out a loud sigh.

"That bad, huh?"

"Worse."

"Oh no. It didn't get violent did it? Did you hit her? Did she hit you? She better not have hit you."

Ali stretched out on the bed. Sitting in a booth all day with just two short trips to the restroom didn't do her back any favors. "I'm not sure where to start."

"The beginning, baby doll, is always a good place."

"I literally sat in the donut shop all day long because Madison refused to talk to me. I kept hearing your voice in my head telling me not to give up." Ali filled him in on the details of the day including Madison's revelations about Howard and coming out to her parents.

"Oh, honey, I'm so sorry. That was so not what I expected. What did you do?"

"You know me. I cried."

"Baby, I do know you and I've never seen you cry." Charley paused. "Never. Not when any of your girlfriends broke up with you, not when your book hit the best seller list, not when—well, never. But you cried over Madison Parker. Why do you think that is?"

"Guess I was saving it all up for today." Ali searched her memory. She hadn't cried over any other breakup. They were annoying, but never heartbreaking. "Maybe I never really cared when any other relationship broke up. I never thought of that before."

"What are you going to do? Are you coming back home tomorrow?"

What was she going to do? She had messed things up very badly twenty years ago. Was there any coming back from that? If she went home, what then? Would anything change? Could she ever find happiness with someone the way she had once found it with Madison—before she had fucked everything up? "I'm staying here. I'm going to win her back and make up for what I did." Her own words surprised the hell out of her.

"I thought you said she was really angry. Do you think she would even be open to that idea?"

Ali thought about it before answering. "I won't know until I try. All I can do is my best. That doesn't mean the tide will turn in the direction I want it to. But maybe it will. Who knows?" Ali spoke without thinking, as if the words and viewpoint were being given to her. "See, that's the thing. We don't know. Not really. No one knows. Because one step in a different direction by any of the key players changes the whole outcome of the play. The ending is not written. It's being written as we live it. The main thing is to be a part of the performance and learn and grow from it."

"Whoa. That's deep. I'm impressed."

"I changed the course of the play when I left. Maybe I can change it back with my return. I know Madison is angry now, but I am going to do everything in my power to change her mind. To get her to forgive me. To give me another chance."

They talked for another twenty minutes, until exhaustion overtook Ali. She fell asleep with the phone by her side, smelling of donuts and dreaming of ways to get Madison to forgive her. She was determined to do just that, no matter how long it took.

❖

"So, Ali showed up here yesterday," Madison said to Jenny as soon as she walked in.

Jenny set her folder on the table and slid into the booth. "What?"

Madison poured them each a cup of coffee. "Yep. Showed up and spent the whole day in that booth over there." Madison nodded in the direction of the booth. "I may have to get a priest in here to do an exorcism on it."

"Did she say anything to you or just sit there?"

"Oh no. She had plenty to say." Madison filled her in. "Can you believe her nerve?"

"Sounds like she was really sorry," Jenny said.

Not the response Madison was expecting. "Sorry? She should be sorry. She threw away something very special."

"Maddy, I'm not arguing with you. Just seems like you are reacting really strongly to this. It all happened so long ago."

"Yesterday wasn't that long ago, Jen." She set her coffee cup on the table with a thud.

Jenny pointed to the cup. "That's kind of what I mean. You have every right to not want her here, but geez, you are just so angry. Should you be this mad?"

Jenny wasn't helping. If she was trying to get Madison to be *less angry* this wasn't the way to do it. She wanted this conversation to be over. She wanted her life to be the way it was before Ali showed up.

"Did you order more napkins?" Madison asked.

"Way to change the subject."

Madison ignored the comment. Jenny obviously got the point because she dropped the subject and got down to donut shop business. They were just finishing up when Valerie arrived for her shift. Madison slipped out of the booth, put her hands on her back just above her hips, and leaned back. She had spent her Sunday off two days ago gardening. She was paying for it now. One more thing to add to her *my life is shitty* list for the week.

"You okay?" Valerie asked her.

"Yeah. I overdid it a couple of days ago. I bend over to plant my flowers, then I'm confused as to why I hurt. My brain still thinks I'm in my twenties. My body strongly disagrees," Madison said.

"Oh, I know that feeling," Valerie sympathized. She couldn't have been more than twenty-four. Madison was sure she had no idea what it was like.

Madison let out a small laugh. It felt good to laugh. To push thoughts of Ali out of her head, if only for a few moments.

"I'm going to get going," Jenny said. "Try not to let this get to you."

"I'm trying. But I have every reason—" She stopped. No sense beating a dead horse, even if that horse was Ali. And she deserved to be beat. She laughed at herself.

"What?" Jenny asked.

"Nothing. Just my brain. Nothing to worry about."

"Should I be worried about your heart?"

"Nope. I've got it under control. I'm going to point my nose forward and live my life without looking back." She said it with more confidence than she felt. "Watching Grayson today?" Madison asked.

"Yes. That little guy fills my cup and drains it at the same time."

"I hear that," said Valerie, the young single woman who, to the best of Madison's knowledge, didn't have any young kids in her life.

Madison laughed again. She was determined to make this a good day, no matter what had happened yesterday. Yesterday was history, just like what happened twenty years ago was history. If you don't learn from it, you repeat it—or however that saying went. One thing was for sure, she didn't ever want to repeat it. It was far too painful the first time around. "Give that kiddo a kiss from Aunt Maddy."

"I will. You okay now?"

"Absolutely." She meant it. If the anger seeped back in, she would just shake it off. She could manage that. Couldn't she?

"Good. I'll see you tomorrow." Jenny turned the OPEN/ CLOSED sign around on her way out the door.

The day was pretty much like any other day, except for back twinges here and there. Thoughts of Ali came and went without much emotion attached to it. Of course, every time someone walked in the door Madison looked up with a sudden flood of acid in her stomach, and each time she was relieved it wasn't Ali. Madison assumed she would be on her way back to wherever it was she had come from.

Ali gave Madison a couple of days to calm down before she attempted to speak to her again. She had no idea where Madison lived, and her online searches didn't prove helpful. She drove by her old house but had heard that both of Madison's parents had passed away. It had been the only time she had the urge to reach out to her since that fateful day. She hadn't of course, but how she wished now that she had. The name on the mailbox was Tina and Bruce Timberland, so that was a dead end.

That left her two choices. She could hang out on the trail she had seen Madison running down while she was parked in front of the donut shop a few days ago or go back to the donut shop. She had no idea how often Madison went running and was sure Madison could easily outrun her if she wanted to get away. So, the donut shop it was.

Going to her place of business again wasn't ideal. But there didn't seem to be any other options. She parked a block away, not that she thought anyone would recognize her car, but she didn't want to take any chances. Each step she took increased the tight feeling in her chest as she walked to O's. She half expected to have a heart attack before she got there. She wondered if she did and Madison came across her, would she just walk over her and leave her there, dying on the sidewalk. The old Madison wouldn't have. But this one—this one probably would. That hurt Ali's heart because she knew she was to blame for Madison hating her.

A few deep breaths outside the door helped loosen her chest. Slightly. Once inside, she spotted Madison at the counter having an animated conversation with two older gentlemen. One of them had his hand on the other's knee. Much too intimate a gesture for them to be just friends. Ali figured they must be partners. There were no other customers in the place. Coming between the breakfast and lunch lull had been a good idea.

The smile on Madison's face disappeared as soon as she spotted Ali. The men at the counter obviously noticed because they both turned and looked at her and then back at Madison.

Madison whispered something to them. Ali couldn't make it out.

"You've got this," one of them said to her. She must have told them who Ali was. With that, they got up and went to the door. Ali stepped out of their way. The taller man nodded at her as way of a greeting.

"I know you probably don't want to see me," Ali started as soon as the door closed behind the men. "But if you could just give me a few minutes, I would really appreciate it."

Madison wiped her hands on the apron wrapped around her waist. "You're right. I don't want to see you. I'll give you a chance to say your piece. But only because my friends said I should. I'm hoping you will leave town after I do."

Leaving wasn't part of the plan. At least she hoped it wasn't. "Would you...I mean—"

"Ali, just spit it out."

"Would you consider having dinner with me? Or a drink? I don't even know if you drink. I mean, if you drink." She knew she was rambling but had trouble reeling it back in.

"Why would I want to do that? I said everything I had to say."

"There is still more I would like to say, and I would like to get to know you again. I never stopped caring. We've missed so much."

"We missed it because of you."

Ali didn't expect this to be easy and it certainly wasn't. She should have prepared better. "I know that now. I take full responsibility. But I'm asking for a chance. I don't expect forgiveness."

Forgiveness. That was an interesting word. Madison knew that she had to forgive Ali, not for Ali's sake but for her own. She just wasn't ready to do it yet. Both Tom and Joe had noticed the look on Madison's face when Ali walked in and immediately asked her what was wrong. She could only guess that she had turned ash white. They had suggested she hear Ali out. That was the only reason she was listening to her now. She wondered what they would say about her agreeing to dinner. She was sure they would be all for it. They were always trying to push her to date. Not that this would be a date. Maybe a compromise would work and get her some peace back in her life. "If I agree to have a drink with you—one drink—will you leave town?"

She could almost see the wheels turning in Ali's head as she thought about it. "Two drinks and you have to give me time to say my piece and be willing to answer questions."

"I reserve the right to refuse any questions that I don't want to answer."

"Deal. When and where?"

Oh shit. Had she really just agreed to have a drink—correction, two drinks—with the woman who had ripped her heart to shreds? If it meant Ali would go home and leave her alone it would be worth it. She could put up with her for an hour or two if that was her reward.

"Tomorrow at seven." The sooner the better. Where was what she wasn't sure of. This was such a small town. Everyone knew everyone, and she didn't want anyone asking her questions if they happened to see her out with Ali. Hell, there were still more than a handful of people in town that they had gone to high school with. She only knew one bar that wasn't right in town. She'd had a few bad internet dates there. They'd soured her on those dating apps.

"There is a bar on Highway Eight. It's called the Butterfly Bar." Madison pulled an order pad from under the counter, wrote down the directions, and handed it to Ali.

"I've never heard of this place."

The comment pissed Madison off. "Ali, you haven't been back here for twenty years. How the hell would you have heard of it?"

"Touché. I deserve that."

Madison refused to feel bad for her statement or for the tone of her voice. Ali did deserve that and much more. "If there is nothing else, I need to get ready for the lunch crowd."

"There is one more thing."

Of course, there was. "What?" she asked, less than patient.

"Can I get a chocolate cream donut? The one I had here the other day was even better than the ones I used to get when I hung out here after school."

The statement threatened to ping Madison's heart, but she pushed the memory away before it could weasel its way in. She boxed up a donut, handed it to Ali, and waved away the money she attempted to hand her.

Valerie came in through the back door for her afternoon shift. She looked from Madison to Ali. "Everything okay here, boss?"

"Yep. Fine. Ali was just leaving," Madison told her.

"Yes. I was just leaving. Thanks for this." Ali held up the donut box, took a couple of steps backward, then turned and made her way out of the shop.

"You sure you're okay?" Valerie asked once Ali was gone. "You seemed pretty upset the last time she was here."

"Yes. I'm fine."

"Can I ask you who that is?"

"My ex," Madison said without emotion. "Long story." She hoped Valerie would drop it and was glad when she didn't ask any more questions. But it wasn't Valerie's possible questions that were bothering her. It was that she had agreed to meet Ali at Butterfly's. Why in the hell had she done that?

CHAPTER EIGHT

Madison got to the Butterfly Bar a half hour early. She wanted to have a drink before Ali got there to calm her nerves. She wasn't sure what she was nervous about. Ali should be the one who was nervous. She was about to state her case and then be sent on her way. Madison refused to be sucked in by her. Sure, they had a past. A past that was wonderful up until the time Ali disappeared. There was no going back now. No making up for lost time.

She ordered her whiskey sour at the bar and made her way to a table in the corner with her drink in hand. She wanted to be sure she could see the door. The last thing she needed was to have Ali sneaking up on her.

It occurred to her that she and Ali had never had a drink in a bar together. Sure, they drank a bottle of beer or two at parties, but they were too young to legally get into bars. Ali, always the more adventurous one, wanted to get fake IDs and go out drinking. But Madison was too chicken, and Ali said she wouldn't go without her. That was one thing Ali always was—loyal. It would have been nice if she realized that Madison was equally as loyal and never would have done anything to hurt her.

Madison watched two women across the bar slow dancing to a song on the jukebox. This was the only gay bar within a hundred miles, and she liked the fact that they didn't play ear-splittingly loud music. You could hear if you wanted to have a conversation. Not that she wanted to have a conversation with Ali. But at least it would go quicker if they weren't constantly asking each other to repeat themselves.

She was surprised to see Ali arrive twenty minutes early. Madison had barely started her drink. She took a large gulp before waving Ali over. "You're early."

Ali laughed. "Look who's talking."

Madison couldn't help but smile and then was mad at herself for doing it. "Grab yourself a drink at the bar. They take forever here if you wait for someone to come to the table."

"Can I get you another one?" Ali pointed to Madison's glass. "I'm fine."

Ali made her way to the bar and returned in short order with a beer in her hand from one of the local microbreweries. Just like old times, although back then their beer was usually the cheapest one available. "Thank you for agreeing to meet me. I have to say I'm surprised it's a gay bar. I didn't know they had such things around here."

"You mean in these here back wood hills. We ain't nearly as uncultured as you remember," Madison said, trying to do a hillbilly accent and failing at it.

"You ain't?" Ali asked.

"We ain't. Besides," Madison said. "If you noticed, we aren't in the small town of Clyde anymore."

"Not too far out though. It's good. I'm glad." Ali pulled out the chair across from Madison and sat down. "Madison, I didn't leave because we lived in a small town. I left because I couldn't face being here without you. I thought we were over. I couldn't bear the thought of seeing you with someone else."

"But—"

Ali put up her hand to stop her. "I know I was wrong, but I didn't know that then. My intention was never to hurt you. It was to try to put the pieces of my broken heart back together somewhere else. Somewhere far away."

"How come you never bothered to tell me you were leaving? Tell me what you thought you saw? Gave me a chance to tell you what happened?" Madison had had no intention of asking these or any other questions. Maybe it was the alcohol, but suddenly she needed to know. Ali's heart hadn't been the only one shattered.

Ali took a swig of her beer and shook her head. "I should have. I thought I knew everything I needed to know when I saw you kissing Howard."

"When you saw Howard kissing me," Madison said a little more harshly than she intended to.

"I didn't know that. I thought you didn't care about me anymore. I was a stupid teenager."

"You didn't give even one thought about what that would do to me? To have you disappear and never talk to me again?"

"If you want an honest answer, in that moment I didn't care."

"Gee, thanks." It might have been honest, but that didn't stop it from hurting.

"No. It's not that I didn't care about you. I've always cared about you. It's that my pain outweighed anything I thought you might be going through. I thought you had moved on. I didn't think you would miss me."

"Miss you? Miss you? You've got to be kidding me. We did everything together. Everything. And then suddenly you're gone. No explanation. No good-bye. Just gone. I cried myself to sleep for months." That was so much more than she had intended to share, but it felt good to get it out.

"I'm so sorry for that. If it helps any, I cried for months too."

"It doesn't."

"Am I going to be punished for the rest of my life for something I did when I was eighteen?"

Madison was silent. If everyone got punished forever for things they did as teenagers, we would all be in a world of trouble. Most teenagers didn't think about consequences, didn't think about the damage they could be doing. She wasn't sitting across from a teenager now. She was sitting across from an adult. An adult who honestly seemed to be sorry. It left her confused, as if her younger, hurt self was warring with her grown-up self who had moved on.

"I've done a lot of stupid things in my life, but that was by far the worse. We both ended up hurt because I didn't give you a chance to explain."

"And there's the difference. I am giving you a chance for just that."

"Don't you think I know that? I appreciate it. After our conversation in the donut shop, I thought for sure you would rather shoot me than listen to anything I had to say."

"I haven't ruled that out yet." Madison laughed. She did her best to suppress it, but it bubbled out anyway.

"Madison, if I thought it would take away any of the hurt, I would load the gun and hand it to you."

"Don't try to cheer me up."

This time it was Ali who laughed. The lines around her eyes crinkled, showing her age, but looking good on her all the same.

This wasn't the way Madison had expected the evening to go. She had imagined sitting across from Ali, stone-faced, while Ali said what she had to say, and that would be it. Over and done and Ali would leave. A big part of her still wanted Ali to leave, but another part, a confusing part, didn't.

"Can I ask you about your life?" Ali took a long swig of her beer, her eyes never leaving Madison while she waited for her answer.

"That depends on the question."

"You said you told your parents you were gay. How did they react?"

Madison had been scared to death to tell them, but she did in order to live her truth as well as to please Ali. A lot of good it did for that. "Both of them said they just wanted me to be happy. They worried but took it well."

"When you told them did you also tell them we had been together?"

"No."

"Why?"

"Because I thought you should have the chance to tell your parents first. Then you were gone."

It all came back to that. Ali left when she should have stayed. Ali had no way to undo the past. All she could do was try to make it up to Madison now. "What about after I was gone?" she asked.

"What about it?" Madison sighed. "You mean did I tell them then?"

Ali nodded. She lifted her beer to her lips and realized the bottle was empty. How had she drained it so fast?

"They thought I was sad because my best friend left town. And I was. You were my best friend as well as the love of my life," Madison said.

Love of my life. Ali rolled those words around in her head. That was why she was never happy or fully committed to anyone else. Because Madison had been the love of her life too. Maybe she still was. How did you replace something like that? Yes, they were young, but the feelings were real. "Do you still feel that way?"

Madison looked confused. "What way?"

"That I was the love of your life?"

"At the time I did."

"That's not what I asked. I asked if you still feel like I was the love of your life. Has there been anyone else you've been with who has compared to what we had?"

"What difference does that make now?"

"Madison, I have had failed relationship after failed relationship. I've come to the conclusion that it's because I never stopped caring about you."

"Ali, that was a long time ago. You need to let it go and get on with your life."

Madison wasn't making this easy, but Ali was determined to find out if she had a chance, even a tiny one, of getting Madison back. "Are you with anyone now?" That would definitely throw a monkey wrench in the plan.

"That doesn't matter. My feelings for you changed a long time ago."

That one hurt. Knife planted directly to her heart and twisted. "But we have now. Maybe you can get the feelings back. Can't we at least try?"

"No."

One simple answer. One word. The worst word Ali had ever heard. Was it worth begging? As much as she wanted to, she knew it would send Madison further away.

"You said you would leave after a drink and conversation. I still expect you to do that," Madison said.

"Two drinks."

"What?"

"You agreed to two drinks."

"Are you really going to push this?"

As much as Ali wanted to stay longer, say more, she knew it was useless. "You win. I'll go." She pushed her chair away from the table. "It was good seeing you, Madison. I hope you're happy. That's all I ever wanted for you. I was just hoping it would be with me." She turned and left before Madison had a chance to respond.

She knew she had to get over Madison. She just didn't know how she was going to do it.

CHAPTER NINE

The donut shop was busier than usual at four o'clock, and Madison stayed a half hour longer than she usually did on a Friday even though Valerie had arrived on time to relieve her. She didn't mind. She didn't have anyone at home waiting for her or anything special planned for the evening. The sun was still bright in the sky as she slipped out the back door. One more reason she loved where she lived. The sunny days far outnumbered the overcast ones. She briefly considered a quick run before dinner time and changed her mind because her back was bothering her again. Just as she opened the door to her car, she heard a voice behind her that made her jump.

"I'm sorry. I didn't mean to startle you."

It was Ali. Of course, it was Ali. Why would Madison have assumed she left, even after she said she would.

"What do you want?" Madison said in the least angry voice she could manage.

"I came to say good-bye. I'm heading back to Syracuse tomorrow morning."

"Have a nice trip." Madison unlocked her car with her key fob. The longer Ali stayed in town the more Madison feared some of her feelings for Ali would return. There were little jabs of it here and there—ordering the donut, seeing Ali with a bottle of beer like when they were young, even Ali saying she was sorry numerous times. They were small things, but they brought Madison back to better times. She wanted—no, needed—to let all that go.

"There's something I'd like to say." Ali looked like she was close to tears.

Madison almost felt sorry for her. Almost. "Then say it quick. I want to get home." Even giving her a few more minutes of her time was more than she wanted to do. Madison had no intention of making this easy on her.

Ali hesitated. "I know I messed up. I'm so sorry. I just wanted to tell you that one more time."

"Okay. Have a nice trip back."

Ali plowed on. "I never stopped caring about you. I hope you can find it in your heart to forgive me. I just wanted to say good-bye. I'll leave in the morning like I promised I would."

Madison opened her car door and got in. She reached for the door handle and stopped. Something pulled in her back. She twisted slightly in the seat trying to adjust it. The sharp pain that ripped through her took her breath away.

Ali continued to talk, but Madison wasn't taking in her words. She was consumed by the pain.

"All right. I can see by the look on your face that you're ready to be rid of me. I hope you can find it in your heart to someday—"

"Stop," Madison managed to squeak out.

"Okay." Without another word, Ali turned and started to walk away.

"Stop," Madison said again.

Ali turned, confused. "I did stop. I'm going."

"I'm—" Madison started, then stopped.

"You're what? I'm leaving like you wanted me to," Ali said.

"I can't move."

"What?"

"I felt something pull in my back. I can't move."

"You threw your back out?" Ali asked.

"Yes," Madison said through gritted teeth.

Ali reached the car in two steps. "What can I do?"

"My phone is in my back pocket. I can't reach around to get it. Go inside and tell someone to come out and help me." She would have Valerie call Jenny. Jenny could help her get home.

"I'm here. I'll help you."

"Go inside."

"I'm right here. I can get your phone for you."

"I don't want you anywhere near my ass."

"Stop being ridiculous." Ali reached behind Madison. "Hold still."

"Like I have a choice."

Madison closed her eyes against the pain as Ali gingerly slid her hand between the seat and Madison. "Are you having fun?" Madison said, not trying to hide the sarcasm her voice. "It's in the other pocket."

"Telling me that sooner would have been nice."

"I thought you would appreciate a free feel."

"Actually, I did. Thanks." She pulled her hand out and triumphantly waved the phone in the air. "Got it."

Madison couldn't believe she was in this predicament and the person who came to her rescue was Ali. "Can you hand it to me please?" Madison stretched out her arm to get it and was rewarded with a shooting pain through her spine. She sucked in a breath. "No, wait. Wait. Don't move."

"Um, you're the one moving."

"Very funny." Not.

"What should I do?" Ali asked.

Madison lowered her arm to her side in slow motion. "You need to call my sister for me."

"Okay. What's the number?" She paused. "In contacts. I know. What's your pass code?"

It occurred to Madison that Ali could look at whatever she wanted to on her phone if she gave her the code. Not that she had anything to hide. She just didn't want Ali knowing any of her business.

"Pass code? Madison?"

"Okay. Okay." She didn't have a choice. "Zero, four, two, nine."

"Your birthday. Clever."

So, Ali remembered her birthday. It could have touched her heart, but it pissed her off instead. She didn't want Ali knowing her birthday or anything else about her. "Just call her."

Ali did as she was told. "It went to voice mail. Should I leave a message?"

"Let me do it." Ali put the phone up to Madison's face. "…available. Leave a message and I'll call you back." Beep.

"Jenny, I have a problem. I threw my back out. I'm kind of stuck in my car at the shop. Call me back. I'm not sure what to do here."

Ali hit the end button. "I can take you to the hospital or home or wherever you need to go."

"Nope. That's okay. I'll wait for Jenny to call me back."

"You're going to sit in your car unable to move for God knows how long? Madison, that doesn't make any sense. I know you're mad at me, but let me help you."

"Go inside and get Valerie. She can drive me home." Madison knew the chances of the shop being slow enough for Valerie to leave Ellie alone were slim. Ellie was just too inexperienced, and Lea mentioned a concert she was going to, so they couldn't call her in.

Ali disappeared, going around the front of the building instead of letting herself in the back door. She emerged with

Valerie in tow a minute later. As Madison had expected, the shop was busy. "I can either drive you or watch the shop," Ali said. "I used to help out when we were kids. I know my way around the place."

Madison shook her head and sucked in another breath. Even that hurt. "No, everything's different now. That's not going to work." She was running out of options here. "You can drive me home. But I'm going to need help getting into the passenger seat."

"I'll pull my car around. It would be easier if I park close and you just go from one car to the other," Ali said.

Madison didn't want to admit it, but that was a better idea. "All right."

It took several minutes and lots of stopping, but they got Madison out of her car and into Ali's. Ali gently buckled the seat belt around her. "Where to?" Ali asked.

"Home. Take a right out of the parking lot."

"Are you sure that's a good idea? Maybe you should go to urgent care or the emergency department."

"I just need to rest it and take some meds. I want to go home." The last thing she needed was to sit in a waiting room for hours.

Ali followed her directions and pulled into Madison's driveway. Getting out of the car with just Ali to help her was going to be more of a challenge. Ali came around to Madison's side and bent over her to unbuckle her belt, which would have made more sense if she'd done it before she had gotten out of the car. Madison held her breath as Ali leaned across her and wondered if Ali had done that on purpose.

Crap, Ali thought as she leaned across Madison. *I should have unbuckled this from the other side. Madison's going to think I'm a jerk.* "Now what?" she asked as she extracted herself from the car.

"Let me see if I can get out by myself." Madison cringed as she attempted to swing her legs out. "I guess I need help."

"Ya think?"

"Never mind. I don't need your attitude. Just leave me. I'll figure out how to get inside."

Ali immediately regretted her words. "Sorry. It's obvious that you can't do this alone. And besides, I can't leave you here. It's my car."

"Good point. Can you help me get my feet on the ground? Slowly."

Slowly was right. It took almost five minutes of starts and stops to get Madison out of the car. Ali put her arm around Madison's shoulders and helped her maneuver into the house, thankful that there was only one small step. She tried her best to ignore the feeling of having Madison so close.

She helped lower Madison onto the couch and adjusted a pillow behind her. "Pain meds?" Ali asked her.

"Yes. For sure."

"Where?"

"Upstairs bathroom, medicine cabinet. It's the only prescription in there. This happened once before. Although not nearly this bad."

Ali spotted the stairs, found the bathroom, and got the medicine with no problem. She was back in the living room in a matter of seconds. She read the label on the bottle before handing it to Madison. "Um, when was the last time this happened? Because this expired five years ago."

"Shit. It's probably still good? Right?"

"I flunked out of medical school, but my common sense says no. You should get a new prescription. Can you call your doctor? I can go pick it up for you."

"You went to medical school?"

Ali laughed. "No. I was just kidding. You know I wanted to be a writer." Ali realized that they didn't know anything about each other anymore. Ali didn't even know if Madison had a significant other. Probably not or she would have had Ali call her instead of Jenny. Unless Madison didn't want her to know she had a significant other. Yeah. She really didn't know much about Madison's life anymore. That was something she would regret for the rest of her life—all the time they had missed out on.

"Did you become a writer?"

"We can talk about that later." Ali hoped there would be a later for them—at least to talk. "Let's call your doctor."

Ali made the call and put the phone on speaker for Madison. Her doctor said the old medicine wouldn't hurt her but also might be less than effective. She called in a new script to the drug store a few blocks away. Ali googled back pain. "We need to ice your back. Do you have an ice pack?" Ali was on her feet heading to what she assumed was the kitchen even before Madison answered.

"I don't think so."

The online article had several suggestions for a makeshift replacement. She found a bag of peas in the freezer. Perfect. She grabbed the dishtowel that was hanging on the oven door and returned to Madison. "Can you move forward a little, so I can put this behind you?"

Madison did as she was told and directed Ali to where the pain was.

"Twenty minutes." Ali looked at her phone. "It's five fifteen now. If I'm not back take the ice off at five thirty-five."

"Okay."

"Anything else before I go?"

Madison shook her head.

Ali ran out to get the medicine and an ice pack. She stopped at Burger King to grab food. The doctor said she shouldn't take the medicine on an empty stomach. If memory served, Madison liked cheeseburgers, no mustard, fries, and vanilla milkshakes. Ali felt funny letting herself into Madison's house, but of course she had no other choice. She found Madison in the same exact position she had left her in. "How ya doing?"

"Same. I'm afraid to move."

Ali held up the bag in her right hand. "Food." And then her left. "Drugs. Which do you want first?"

"Drugs. Glasses are in the cupboard on the left side of the sink in the kitchen."

Madison downed two pills in one gulp. She was quiet as she picked at her food. "How are you feeling?" Ali asked after she cleaned up. The pained look on Madison's face had eased up. The meds must have kicked in.

"Better. Thanks. I'm okay now. You're free to return to your life. I appreciate your help."

As much as she hated to admit it, Madison meant it, she did appreciate Ali's help. It didn't change anything, but she would have been stranded, still sitting in her car, unable to move if it wasn't for Ali. With the pain eased up a bit, Madison attempted to stand, but quickly gave up. Too soon.

"What do you need? I'll get it for you," Ali asked.

"Nothing. I thought maybe I can go upstairs after you go and lie down."

"I can help with that. Do you think the stairs will be too much?"

"Never mind." The last thing she wanted was Ali helping her to her bedroom. "I'm fine here."

"Are you going to spend the night on the couch? I don't think you'll be very comfortable."

That wasn't a bad idea. It would solve the problem of getting upstairs alone. "Yes. I think I will."

"Okay. What do you sleep in? I'll go get your night clothes and help you get into them."

"Yeah. I'm thinking no. You will not be doing that." No way. No how.

"I can do it with my eyes closed." Ali stood, put her arms out in front of her—resembling a zombie—and closed her eyes. "See. No sweat." She took a couple of steps forward and smashed her shin on the coffee table. "Ow. Damn."

Madison did her best to suppress a laugh. The stunt brought Madison back to when they were young, and Ali was always doing something silly to make her laugh. She pushed the memory aside.

It occurred to her that Jenny hadn't called her back. "Let's try calling Jenny again."

Ali rubbed her leg where she bumped it. "Sure." She used Madison's phone and put it on speaker. It went directly to voice mail. "She must have her phone off."

Damn. The meds were starting to make her sleepy. "Ali, you can go. I'm going to sleep on the couch. I'll be fine." She would be fine except for the fact that she had to pee. Just the thought of trying to get on and off the toilet by herself sent a moment of panic through her. The last time this happened she was out of commission for three days. Patty, Jenny's daughter, had helped her out while Jenny filled in for her at the donut shop. Of course, that was before Patty worked and before she had a baby, now two years old, to chase after. She would figure this out. Jenny would call her back sooner or later. She could manage until then. Her bladder disagreed. Damn bladder.

"Madison, are you sure? I don't mind staying till Jenny calls back."

"I…um…well, I need to go to the bathroom."

"Okay. Sure. How should we do this?"

Madison thought about it for a minute. It might be better to pee her pants and ruin her couch than to die of embarrassment. She wasn't even sure she could pull her own underwear down.

She was sorry she'd said anything as soon as the words were out of her mouth. "Never mind. I'm going to wait for Jenny."

"Madison."

"What? I can hold it."

"I get the message. Okay. I'll go." Ali picked Madison's phone up from the coffee table and typed. "I just put my number in your phone. Call me if you need me. Is it okay if I copy Jenny's number so I can check in with her to see how you're doing?"

"You didn't send yourself a text from my phone, so you had my number?" That's what Madison would have done.

"No. I didn't think you would want me to have your number. I was trying to be respectful."

"I appreciate that." Madison rattled off Jenny's number. It was the least she could do seeing as Ali had been a real life saver. "Thank you again for all your help. I'll be fine."

Ali nodded. "I'll let myself out. Do you want me to lock the door?"

No one locked their doors in this small town. It was probably one of the few towns in America where people still trusted their neighbors. "No, it's fine. Have a good night." Madison hoped that last line didn't sound like she was pushing Ali out. Which was exactly what she was trying to do.

"You too. Call me if you need me," Ali repeated. Madison was sure she wouldn't. Ali let herself out. Madison waited until she heard the door close before she attempted to get up to use the bathroom. No matter how slowly she moved, it hurt. She grabbed her phone from the arm of the couch where Ali left it and slipped it into her front pocket. She made it to the bathroom and managed to get her pants down and onto the toilet. She did her business and attempted to get up. There was nothing to hold onto to give her leverage except the toilet paper holder and that wasn't very helpful. She called Jenny again. No answer. She tried Jenny's daughter, Patty. No answer.

"Son of a bitch." She called Ali.

"Hello."

"It's Madison."

"Madison? Are you okay?"

"This is either hilarious or a tragedy. Either way it's probably the most embarrassing situation I've ever been in." She hesitated, knowing she didn't have a choice but to tell Ali what the problem was. "I'm stuck on the toilet."

There was no laugh or even a giggle like she expected. "I'll be right there," Ali said.

It took her only a few minutes to return. "Madison?" she called after letting herself in.

"In here."

"Marco."

Madison smiled despite her situation and embarrassment. "Polo."

Ali stuck her head in the open door. "Hi."

Madison felt her face flush with heat. She was sure she must be beet red.

"I hear you've got a bit of trouble."

"You could say that. I didn't know what else to do."

"I'm glad you called me. Can I come in?"

"Not sure how we are going to do this otherwise."

Ali slipped her arms around Madison and eased her up. Once she was in a standing position, Ali helped her pull up her underwear and pants, keeping her eyes focused on Madison's face. Madison appreciated that.

Ali helped her to the couch. "I think I should stay here tonight. Or at least until Jenny can come."

Madison was in no condition to argue. "How about we give those pills a little more time to work and then you can decide if you want me to help you upstairs or if you want to sleep on the couch. I can help you get your pajamas on then."

"Okay." What else could she say? Maybe if the pills kicked in enough, she could get ready for bed herself. She doubted it.

"Want the TV on or anything? Or maybe I could sing to you," Ali said.

She smiled. Another memory filtered in. Ali would sing to her whenever she was down. The thing was, Ali couldn't sing to save her life. She often sang even worse on purpose to make Madison laugh. It never failed. "Yeah, no thanks. I don't think my eardrums can take it."

"Oh, come on. I never sang that bad. You used to love it." Ali smiled.

"I did," Madison admitted. "But I was young and foolish then. Now I'm all grown up and sophisticated."

"Well, excuse me, Your Highness. I didn't realize you had risen so high in the world."

Madison was glad they were keeping it light. She didn't think she could stand the thought of one more heartfelt apology. Of course, at some point she should probably tell Ali she forgave her. But tonight was not the time for that.

"I have. TV would be fine. That won't hurt my back."

"Oh, and me singing will?" Ali picked up the TV remote from the coffee table.

"Probably not, but why take the chance?"

"I can't sing, don't ask me," Ali sang, letting her voice purposely crack.

Madison giggled. She wasn't sure if it was because Ali was being silly or because she was feeling loopy because of the pills. "Ow. Don't make me laugh. It hurts."

"Sorry."

That word again. Enough. "No more apologies tonight."

"If I understand this, there will be no more singing, no more apologies, and no more making you laugh. Anything else?"

"No. I think that's it for now. Wait, one more. If you do need to help me get ready for bed, no peeking." Oh yeah, the drugs were affecting more than her pain level.

"I wouldn't dream of it. Well, I have actually dreamt of it, but I will do my best to grant your wish."

"You haven't changed much." Madison surprised herself with that statement.

"That's where you're wrong. I've changed a great deal." Ali sat down, remote in hand.

"You still have that silly sense of humor. How have you changed?" Ali seemed to turn serious. "I've grown up in a lot of ways. But, interestingly enough, I have realized in the last few weeks that I have been so immature in other ways."

"Immature how?"

"In relationships. None of them after you worked. But I stayed in them until the other person kicked me out of them. I was like a child hoping to be loved, never realizing that I didn't really want any of these women to love me." She shook her head. "I'm probably not making much sense."

"I wasn't sure if it was you or the pills. They seem to be talking to me too." Madison giggled. "Sorry."

"You get to say sorry, but I don't?"

"Sorry for saying sorry. Oh yeah. I guess I do get to say it."

"Maybe we should get you to bed."

"I had a comeback line for that, but it went out of my head."

"You should say something like, yes, take me to bed."

"Nice try, but I'm thinking no. At least saying it like that. My head is starting to swim, but the good news is the pills took the edge off my pain. At least while I'm sitting. No guarantees to what will happen when I stand up and try to walk."

Ali got up. "Should I get your stuff, and we can get you ready down here, or should we try for the stairs and get you up to your bedroom?"

"Help me stand up and let's see how I do with that first." She put her hand out to Ali. "Please."

Ali took her hand and wrapped an arm around her. She eased her up to a standing position. "How was that?"

"Manageable. Let's try the stairs." They took several tentative steps.

"Doing okay?"

"Yep. Just so you know I'll probably start swearing like a sailor if I'm not."

"Oh, man. Not a sailor." They took a few more steps in slow motion.

"Yep. A sailor."

It took a few minutes to get up the stairs, but they did it. There was pain with every step, but it wasn't bad enough to make Madison swear. Ali helped lower her to a sitting position on the bed, and Madison told her where her nightclothes were.

Good thing I'm on drugs, Madison thought, or I would be freaking out at the thought of Ali undressing me.

Ali made quick work of gathering what they needed and was mercifully careful and respectful getting Madison changed.

"The guest room is down the hall and there are extra blankets in the hall closet," Madison said once she was on her feet again and Ali was pulling down the covers for her. Ali helped her into bed and pulled up the blankets.

"Got it." Ali ran downstairs and grabbed the bottle of pills, a glass of water, and Madison's phone. She set the water and pills on the nightstand and fiddled with something on Madison's phone. "I set your alarm for your next dose of meds. It's important to take it on time. It's not good to be chasing the pain."

Madison couldn't have asked for better help. Ali seemed to think of everything, which was good because Madison was having trouble thinking at all. Sleep was overtaking her fast.

"Anything else you need?" Ali asked.

"Mmm…ffe…nnaw."

"I'll take that as a no." Ali brushed the hair away from Madison's face. She resisted the urge to kiss her on the forehead. Oh, who was she kidding? Her attention went to Madison's lips as she drifted off to sleep. It took willpower to not do something stupid. She left the room and turned off the light but left the door open.

Once in the spare bedroom she realized she didn't have anything to sleep in. All her stuff was still at the hotel. She didn't dare leave in case Madison needed something while she was gone. She slipped off her shoes, pants, and socks and shimmied out of her bra without removing her T-shirt.

She doubled up the pillows on the bed and jumped in. She was halfway through a Netflix movie on her phone when she heard Madison's phone ring. She stopped the movie and listened. When it didn't appear that Madison was going to answer it, Ali went into her room and pressed the answer button. It was Jenny. Ali explained what was going on.

"I'm glad she's not alone. I can come over if you want to go."

"I've got this. We can see how she is in the morning. I'm sure she'll give you a call."

"Stay close. That medicine knocks her out. Just make sure you can hear her if she calls. She tends to not be very loud when she is groggy."

"Okay. Anything else I should know?"

"Not really. Sounds like you have things handled. Please make sure one of you keeps me updated."

"Will do." Ali went back to the guest room after she hung up Madison's phone. She grabbed the pillows off the bed and two blankets from the hall closet. She made herself a makeshift bed on the floor. She wanted to make sure she could hear Madison if she needed her. She sent a quick text to Charley, letting him know what was going on and that she would probably be in Maryland a few days longer. She adjusted her pillows, did her best to get into a comfortable position, and lay awake for a long time just listening to Madison breathe. Thoughts of a younger Madison, a Madison who loved her, drifted in and out of her thoughts. She wanted that Madison back. She wanted this Madison now. She wondered if she would ever find another love like the one they'd had. One way or another, she was determined to find that again.

Chapter Ten

Madison woke to pain in her back and the sound of light snoring coming from the vicinity of her floor. It took her several seconds to realize that Ali was sleeping a few feet away. There was enough light from the moon seeping into the room that she could make out her outline and one naked leg sticking out from under the blanket. She still had nice legs for a thirty-eight-year-old. Leg, she jokingly corrected herself. Her other leg might be hideous. She giggled out loud.

"Huh? What?" Ali was awake and on her feet in an instant. "What do you need?"

Turned out that Ali's left leg was just as nice as her right.

"I've got some pain going on here."

"I don't hear you swearing so it can't be that bad."

"I've got some fucking pain going on here. Is that better? Is it time for more medicine?"

Ali looked at Madison's phone. "You've got fifteen minutes, but it's probably okay to take it now."

She helped Madison sit up, propping a pillow behind her. Oh yeah, that hurt. "Fuck."

Madison took the pills and water Ali offered her and downed them. "How come you're sleeping on the floor? There is a perfectly good bed in the other room."

"I wanted to be close by in case you needed me." That went straight to Madison's heart. She didn't know anyone else who would have done that for her. "That was very kind of you."

"Jenny called by the way."

"She did? I never even heard my phone."

"You were pretty out of it. Those pills do you in, but the sleep is good for you." Madison couldn't believe she was thinking it, but she was glad Ali was there to help. It wouldn't change anything, but it was nice having her around for a while.

❖

The pain had let up a little by morning, but each movement still hurt. A lot. Ali helped her downstairs in her pajamas and settled her in on the couch. Ali ran out to get breakfast and her stuff from the motel, while Madison called Jenny.

"I couldn't believe it when Ali answered the phone last night. I thought maybe the two of you were sleeping together," Jenny said.

"Why would your brain even go there?"

"Maddy, I've seen how messed up you have been over her. You must still have feelings for her, even if you won't admit it."

"You don't know what you're talking about." Madison adjusted her position on the couch, with sloth like speed, trying to get more comfortable.

"That's what I'm talking about. You won't admit it, even to yourself. If you were truly over her, then anything she did, including showing up in town, wouldn't have bothered you."

"Whatever." Where was Ali with that food? Madison's brain was starting to swirl again as the last dose of medicine was taking effect. She had never been one to like the feeling of getting high, even in high school when everyone else was smoking pot. She certainly wasn't enjoying this feeling now.

"Anyway, Patty is taking the next three days off so she can stay with the baby. That way I can fill in for you at the donut shop. We can reevaluate after that and see if you need more time off. How does that sound?"

"Good. I really appreciate this."

"No problem. Do you think Ali would be willing to stay with you to help?"

Damn. Madison hadn't even thought about the fact that no one else would be available.

"I don't know." Could she possibly be able to stay by herself? She twisted her back slightly to test the pain level. Even with taking the meds she would have trouble managing by herself. Who else could she ask? She had a few friends. Of course the donut shop kept her so busy that she hadn't kept up with them as much as she should have. Besides, most of them had kids to take care of. She was out of options. "I'll ask her," she said reluctantly. As if on cue, Ali came through the door trying to balance a tray with two cups of coffee, two big bags, and a smaller bag from Burger King. She nodded to Madison, set the tray on the coffee table, and disappeared into the kitchen.

"Ali just got back. I'll ask her about staying to help."

"Okay. Keep me updated on everything. I'll let you go."

They said their good-byes and Madison let her phone drop on the couch cushion next to her. She didn't dare reach for one of the coffee cups on the table in front of her. She didn't have to wait long for Ali to return.

"I picked up some groceries, so we don't have to keep eating fast food. I hope you don't mind."

"That was very nice of you," Madison said, and she meant it. Ali moved the coffee table closer to Madison.

"I'll be right back," Ali said and disappeared out the door only to return with a box. She set the box on the table and put one of the cups of coffee on it. "Cream and two sugars. I hope that's still how you like it. I should have checked before I left."

Madison was touched that Ali had remembered. She was shocked and a bit embarrassed when her eyes welled up with tears. She tried to nonchalantly dab at them with her sleeve.

"Are you in pain? What can I do?" Apparently, the move hadn't escaped Ali's notice.

"I'm okay. Yes. The coffee is perfect."

Ali proceeded to set Madison's breakfast on the box she had put the coffee on. "That should make it easier for you. Less reaching and twisting."

This time the dam opened, and Madison started full-on crying. She was sure it was a combination of pain, medicine, and Ali's unexpected thoughtfulness. Ali's unexpected thoughtfulness also frustrated the hell out of her. She didn't want to be grateful to her. Crap. "Oh, Madison, you're crying."

Madison swiped carefully at the tears on her cheeks. "Your powers of observation are impressive." She immediately regretted her remark, meant to be funny but sounding more like sarcasm. "I'm sorry."

Ali pulled several napkins from the Burger King bag and handed them to Madison. "You have nothing to be sorry for. You have every reason to cry. I just wish there was something more I could do."

That only brought a fresh cascade of tears.

Ali had the urge to put her arms around Madison and pull her into a tight hug, but not only would that cause her more pain, it probably wouldn't be welcomed. "Madison, what can I do?"

Madison wiped her eyes. "Nothing. I'm all right."

"You don't seem all right. Is it the pain?"

"The pain isn't helping. But that's not why I'm crying."

Ali squatted down in front of Madison and looked up at her. "Then what's wrong?"

"Damned if I know." She laughed as if it was the funniest thing ever.

That only managed to confuse Ali more. At least laughing was better than crying.

Ali stood. "Get some food into you. Maybe that will help." Madison nodded.

"Don't cry when I tell you this, but I got you a present."

"You didn't have to do that."

"Don't get too excited. I got you a raised toilet seat. You know, the kind with the handles that old people use. It's in the car."

"I'm too old to use the regular toilet," Madison whined.

"Stop. You shouldn't say you're old. I prefer the word elderly."

"Yeah. That is so much better. And if I'm elderly, you are too. You're only a few months younger than me."

"I accept that. The difference is I can use a regular toilet."

"That is something to celebrate." Madison held up her cup of coffee. "But seriously, I really do appreciate it. I'll reimburse you for whatever you spent."

"My treat."

Madison laughed. "It's the best gift I've ever gotten."

"Wow. You don't lead a very interesting life do you?"

"Apparently not, if a toilet seat can be so meaningful to me."

"Okay, enough toilet talk. I need to get that out of my head so I can enjoy my breakfast."

They ate in relative silence. Ali was in the kitchen cleaning up when she heard the front door open and a female voice ask Madison how she was doing. She didn't know if she should just stay in the kitchen or go back to the living room. Curiosity won out. She recognized Jenny, Madison's older sister, immediately. It had been a long time since she'd seen her last.

"Hi, Ali," Jenny said. "I just stopped in to see how things are going. I've only got about a half hour, then I need to get back to the donut shop."

"Hi. You haven't changed at all." The years looked like they had been kind to her. "I'll leave you two to visit. Madison, do you need anything before I go?"

"You don't have to leave," Jenny said.

"It's okay. I'll be back in about twenty minutes if that's okay. Madison?"

"No. I don't need anything."

"Back soon," Ali said as she headed to the door. She started her car and drove down the street about three blocks. She pulled over and called Charley.

"How are you doing, baby doll?"

"Madison seems to be in a lot of pain, even with the medicine."

"Understandable. Back pain is the worse. But I'm asking how you are doing."

Ali had to think about it for a few moments. She had been so intent on taking care of Madison that she hadn't checked in with herself. "I'm okay. It's so nice and so weird to be around her again."

"Weird how?"

"I never thought I would ever see her again, let alone be in this situation. It feels surreal at times."

"Is that good or bad?"

"Neither. It just is." Ali didn't know how to explain it. Her feelings for Madison had been seeping back in. But Madison had made it perfectly clear that she didn't feel the same. Ali had no choice but to accept that. When Madison felt better Ali would head back home and get on with her life. At least she would be doing it with a better understanding of herself, and her feelings.

"When do you plan on coming home?"

"Miss me?" Ali teased him.

"Always, darling."

"I miss you too. I guess I'll be back as soon as Madison doesn't need me anymore." Not that she wanted Madison to be in pain, but she hoped that wouldn't be too soon.

"Then what?"

"What do you mean?"

"What are you going to do once you get back home?"

"Go back to my life, write, sleep in my own bed, etcetera."

"It's the etcetera that I'm asking about. The purpose of this trip, if you'll recall, was to find out what went wrong with your relationship with Madison Parker so you could have a successful relationship in the future. What are your thoughts on that?"

Charley always got right to the heart of the matter. Sometimes it was helpful. Other times it was a pain in the ass. This time it was the latter. Ali wasn't ready to start another relationship. This trip hadn't gone as planned. She did find out what went wrong with Madison. She found out she had been a jerk. She wasn't sure where to go from here, but she was certain it wasn't into the arms of someone else. She might just be better off never having another relationship. Maybe that's what she had learned. She was no good at connection.

"I think celibacy and loneliness are my best bets."

"You don't mean that, sweetie."

"I do. I blew every relationship I've ever had. I screwed up so badly with Madison that she spent twenty years hating me."

"What happened to your determination to win her back?"

"Pressuring her to give me another chance when she made it clear that she doesn't want that wouldn't be right. I'll stick around to help her out, but that's the end of it. I hope someday she can find it in her heart to forgive me. Maybe someday we can even be friends."

❖

"Scale of one to ten, how bad is the pain?" Jenny asked Madison.

"Without meds it's about an eleven. With meds it's a seven."

"That bad, huh?"

"Yes. That bad." Not the most fun Madison had ever had.

"How about Ali? Is she being helpful? Are you okay having her here?"

"She is an eleven on a scale of one to ten. Your other question is a little more complicated." So many words could describe how Madison felt about having Ali there. Anger. Frustration. Gratitude. Relief. Happiness. Confusion.

"In what way?" Jenny asked.

Madison wasn't sure she could explain it, especially considering she didn't really understand it herself. "I'm grateful for the help. It sort of pisses me off that it's Ali that's helping me."

"I don't know any way around that. We are actually lucky she was here when this happened."

Madison nodded her agreement. If there was anyone else, she could have asked, she surely would have. "I know."

"I can pick up groceries for you when I get done with my shift later. What do you need?"

"I don't think we need anything." We. She never thought she would ever use that word and be including Ali in it again. Life sure was strange sometimes. "Ali stopped and got stuff when she went out to get us breakfast."

"How about medicine?"

"All set there too, thanks to Ali."

"Sounds like she is taking good care of you."

That's what was so frustrating. Madison was finding it harder and harder to remain mad at her. "Yep."

"Want me to drop off donuts when I'm done for the day?"

"Can you bring a few chocolate cream ones for Ali?" It was the least she could do for everything Ali was doing for her.

"You got it."

They were interrupted by a knock on the door. "Are you expecting anyone?" Jenny asked.

Madison shook her head. Jenny opened the door to find Ali standing there.

"Why did you knock?" Madison asked her.

"I didn't want to just barge in," Ali answered.

"Don't be silly. You wouldn't be barging in. Just let yourself in next time." Madison felt weird even as she said the words. She wasn't sure if it was the meds or the fact that she had just invited Ali to come in like she lived there.

"I'm going to get going," Jenny said. "Patty asked if you would be up for a visit from her and Grayson this evening. What do you think?"

"As long as they aren't expecting me to entertain them. I don't think I'm up for doing a jig." Madison smiled. "Of course, they can come."

They said their good-byes and Jenny was on her way.

"Who're Patty and Grayson?" Ali asked after the door closed.

"My boyfriend and his mother."

"Oh."

Madison found it was just as much fun to tease Ali now as it had been when they were in high school. "My boyfriend is two years old, and his mother is Patty, Jenny's daughter."

Was it her imagination or did Ali look relieved?

"By the way," Madison continued. "Jenny wanted me to ask you if you could stay to help for a few more days."

"Jenny wanted to know?"

Madison felt an unexpected blush creep up her neck. "I'm asking too. You can say no if it's inconvenient. I know you were planning on going home. I'm sure you have a life to get back to. I don't even know if you have to get back to a job." Madison knew almost nothing about Ali's life.

"Of course. I'll stay as long as you need me. No job to get back to. I'm waiting on edits from my editor, and I can work on them from anywhere. My next book isn't due for several months."

"So, you did become a writer." Was it wrong that Madison felt proud of her? "I'm proud of you." Guess not. "What kind of books do you write?"

"Crime thrillers."

"Why did you choose that?"

"I've fucked up every romance I've ever had in my life, so that genre seemed out of the question."

Madison didn't know how to respond to that, until Ali laughed, and Madison felt free to laugh as well.

"The main character in my books is a private detective. She's also a lesbian, but that is just a part of who she is. She rarely acts on it."

"And why is that?" Ali hesitated long enough that Madison didn't think she was going to answer at all.

"She was hurt when she was younger and doesn't trust enough to get into another relationship."

"Drawing on your own life?" Even though their breakup had been Ali's fault, Ali obviously had suffered because of it. Of course, Ali had blamed Madison for years thinking she was to blame.

"I'm embarrassed to say yes."

"Why does that embarrass you?" Was that a blush creeping into Ali's cheeks?

"I used my heartache—which proved to be my own fault— as the basis for the character. I think most writers put a piece of themselves into every character."

"Even the bad guys?"

Ali smiled. "Oh yeah. It's fun to pretend to do bad things and try to figure out ways to get away with it. There is a certain joy that comes from the bad guy—or gal—doing something evil or seeking revenge on someone they perceived did them wrong."

Interesting. "Was the character who did them wrong based on me?"

"No comment."

It was as if a switch in Madison's heart had been flipped. Suddenly, she saw things from a different angle. "Ali, I'm sorry you had so much pain around me."

Ali shook her head. "That was my fault."

"That doesn't make what you went through any less painful."

"No. But it did help make me a successful author." Ali smiled. "I managed to get through it."

"Sounds like it clouded much of your life."

Ali thought about it for minute. It had done just that. So much of Ali's life had revolved around that hurt.

Madison interrupted her thoughts. "So, you've done well? With your books?"

"You could say that. I'm able to support myself with my writing. That's not an easy thing for an author to do."

"Ali, that's great."

Madison's approval meant a lot to Ali. More than it probably should have. "Thanks." The alarm on Ali's phone went off, startling her. "Time for another ice pack," she announced. She retrieved the ice pack from the freezer, set it in place on Madison's back, and settled down across from her.

"Do you think it might be time for your main character to find love?"

Ali gave it a moment of contemplation before answering. "No. I don't think she will. She would just mess it up."

"Are you still talking about your character or are you talking about yourself?"

"Now that is an interesting question."

"Isn't it though?" Madison smiled. "That's why I asked it. What is the answer?"

"I don't know."

"Yes, you do. I can tell by the look on your face. You just don't want to admit it."

That surprised Ali. She thought she was covering well, but apparently, Madison could read her. She always could.

"Both I guess."

"Why?"

Ali pulled her phone from her pocket and opened the screen. "Isn't it about time for your next dose of medicine?"

"That can wait five minutes." Madison's voice softened. "Why do you think you would mess it up?"

Ali really didn't want to answer the question. The truth was she was afraid her feelings for Madison would get in the way of letting anyone else in. Telling Madison that just didn't seem right. She formulated her answer very carefully, not wanting to lie, but not willing to reveal everything either. "I've messed up every relationship so far. No reason not to believe that would continue."

"I don't think you are giving yourself enough credit."

That response confused Ali. Was Madison paying her a compliment? She had been so pissed at her only a few days ago.

"Yep. It's time for you next dose of medicine. I'm going to make us lunch. Soup and a sandwich sound good? I'll put the soup in a cup so it will be easier for you." Ali stood.

"I guess that means we're changing the subject?"

"You catch on quick."

"I'm not as stupid as I look."

"There are lots of words I would use to describe you. Stupid isn't one of them." She started for the kitchen.

"I was just funning ya. I ain't no dummy. I is smart. I got me a high school ed-u-ma-cation and ever thang."

Ali stopped and turned around, laughing. "You're smart all right. Lunch and pills coming right up." She continued into the kitchen to make lunch. She smiled the whole time she was warming up the soup. She was really enjoying spending time with Madison. How in the world would she ever be able to leave?

Chapter Eleven

They had just finished supper when there was a knock on the door. "That must be Patty and Grayson," Madison said. "Come on in," she called so Ali wouldn't have to get up.

Patty came in holding Grayson. "Are you up for some company, Aunt Madison?"

"I am always happy to see this little guy. Hi, sweetie," she said to the toddler.

"What about me?" Patty asked.

"You can come in too." Madison waved a hand in Ali's direction. "Patty, this is Ali. She's helping me out." Madison didn't know how much Jenny had told her. She didn't want to get into who Ali was.

They exchanged hellos. Patty set Grayson down and he went running in his wobbly way straight to Ali. "Well, hello there, little guy."

"Hi. Hi. Hi. Hi," he said. He put his arms out to her and she picked him up.

"Oh my God," Patty said. "He never goes to anyone he doesn't know. He must like you. Kids know a good person when they see one."

Madison was just as surprised. It often took him twenty or thirty minutes into a visit for him to warm up to anyone new. He giggled as Ali bounced him on her knee. "What can I say? He has good taste."

"Are you sure you don't have candy in your pocket?" Madison asked.

"Not that I know of. Kids and dogs just seem to like me."

"Not cats?" Patty asked.

"No. Cats don't have good taste like kids and dogs."

"Puppy dog. Puppy dog," Grayson squealed.

"Can he have a c-o-o-k-i-e?" Ali asked Patty, spelling out the word.

"I don't think I have any," Madison said.

"I bought some when I got groceries today. I figured you might have company, seeing as you're laid up. Is it okay, Patty?"

"Sure."

Ali set Grayson on the floor and stood. He reached up with his chubby fingers and wrapped them around Ali's pinky. "You want to come with me, little man?"

Grayson's shock of blond hair bounced as he nodded his head up and down.

Ali glanced at Patty. She nodded. "Anyone else want one?"

"Sure," Patty said. "If you have enough."

Madison shook her head and watched as Ali went into the kitchen with her great-nephew attached to her. It was a sweet sight. "She seems nice," Patty said. "I'm so glad she was able to help you out."

As much as she hated to admit it, Madison was glad too. She would be in a real bind if Ali hadn't been there.

Grayson came running back into the room, balancing cookies in his chubby hands, followed by Ali. Ali sat as Grayson squeaked, "I got cookie, Mama." He handed one to Madison and one to his mother.

"He insisted that Aunt Maddy needed a cookie," Ali told her.

He took his final cookie and attempted to crawl back up on Ali. She lifted him up and set him on her lap. She didn't seem to mind that her pants were being showered with cookie crumbs as he munched away. "It's so nice of you to help Aunt Madison, Ali. I'll bet she's glad you were in town visiting."

Madison was so pissed when Ali first appeared, but she did have to admit to herself that she did appreciate the help. Even if it was Ali who was helping her.

"I'm happy to do it. I'm just sorry she's in so much pain."

"You in pain, Aunt Maddy?" Grayson asked. Madison nodded.

"I kiss your boo-boo." He wiggled his way off Ali's lap and ran to Madison, coming to a stop just short of running into her. He bent slightly and kissed her on the knee. "All better?"

She brushed a hand though his hair. "All better. Thank you so much, sweetie."

He took his place again on Ali's lap. He seemed to be really taken with her. And why wouldn't he be? She was gentle and kind. Kids could pick up on things like that.

Even though it was still fairly early, when Patty and Grayson left, Madison was ready for bed. The medicine didn't seem to be making her loopy, but it was tiring her out—that and the pain, which was better, but still not great.

Ali helped her up the stairs and into the bathroom. Madison was able to stand long enough to brush her teeth and wash her face. Ali helped her with everything else, including settling down in bed. "You don't need to sleep on the floor tonight," Madison told Ali. "If I need you, I'll call you."

"Are you sure?"

"Totally."

"Okay. I'm going to go get the stuff I picked up at the motel from my car. I'll check on you when I come back in."

"Ali, I'm fine. Get your things and settle in. Watch TV, read a book, make yourself a drink, whatever. I'm going to sleep. You need to relax for a while. You've been here for me for the last day and a half. Take some time for yourself."

"It's not a problem. I just want to make sure you're okay."

"I'm okay. Go. Do you for a while."

Ali nodded and started for the door. "Call me if—"

"If I need you. Got it. Go."

Ali disappeared and Madison could hear the front door open and close. Madison replayed the day in her mind, how much help Ali had been and how good she had been with Grayson. Ali had always been so kind and caring when they were together. In her anger, Madison had forgotten about that. Any anger that remained was quickly turning to sadness. How different things might have been if Ali hadn't jumped to conclusions so long ago. She couldn't help but think what kind of life they could have had. Together.

Ali was doing her best to make up for that now, but Madison reasoned that Ali would be just as kind to anyone who needed her. That was the person she used to be, and it was becoming obvious that was the person she still was. Madison's heart softened. She hadn't treated Ali very kindly when she showed up unexpectedly, but that hadn't stopped Ali from helping her. Madison was the one who had been in the wrong. Not only did Ali deserve to be forgiven, she also deserved an apology.

Ali quietly dragged her suitcase upstairs and into the guest room. She could tell by Madison's breathing that she was already asleep. Being in so much pain must be exhausting. She crept back down the stairs, made herself the microwave popcorn she'd bought, and settled down on the couch with the remote. She was still deciding on what to watch when the front door opened, startling her. She turned in time to see Jenny come in.

"Hi. Is Madison in bed already?"

"Yeah. She's out like a light."

"I'm not surprised. I was at the shop much later than I thought I would be. Madison asked me to drop these off for you."

She held up a small box with O's Donuts printed on the side. "Chocolate cream donuts."

"That was so nice of her—and you. Do you want to sit down?" Ali realized how weird that must be, to have Ali invite Jenny to sit down in her own sister's house.

"Sure. I have a few minutes." She set the bag on the coffee table and sat down across from her. Ali could smell the donuts and her mouth watered. The bowl of popcorn next to her paled in comparison.

"I wanted to thank you for sticking around and taking care of Madison. From what Madison tells me you're really helping her."

Ali was glad that Madison thought that. She was doing her best but felt like she fell short at times. She wished she could ease her pain. "I'm happy to do it."

"Madison shared your history and more recent..." Jenny hesitated, seeming to search for the right word. "...events." Ali wasn't surprised.

"I've apologized to Madison. I'm so sor—"

Jenny put her hand up. "I know. I guess I'm just trying to tell you how much I appreciate you being here after everything that happened. Most people would have run back home way before now."

"I doubt that."

"Oh no. They would have. But you stepped up to the plate. You're a good apple in my opinion."

That touched Ali's heart. She expected Jenny, and anyone else Madison told about the situation, to hate her. She was glad Jenny didn't. Patty hadn't acted like she was mad at her either. Jenny only stayed a few minutes more. She explained that she had a husband waiting at home and she was anxious to put her feet up. Ali helped herself to a donut as soon as the door closed behind Jenny. She found some Ziploc bags in a kitchen drawer for the rest. She felt a little bad—but only a little—throwing out the bowl of popcorn but figured it would get stale if she saved it.

Ali turned off the lights, locked the door, and tiptoed up the stairs to check on Madison. She looked so peaceful. And beautiful. Ali stood there longer than she probably should have, just taking her in. She wanted this memory to take back to Syracuse with her when she did have to go.

Syracuse. That seemed so far away and so insignificant. The only thing she had going for her there was Charley. He was the only one who would miss her if she just disappeared one day. Not that she had any plans to do that. She had nowhere else to go. They say you can't go home again and they—whoever they are—were right. This had been her home once. This little town and its people had been important to her. She had left all that behind and they had moved on without her. Nobody would miss her here when she left. That made her more than a little sad.

She got herself ready for bed and slipped under the floral comforter with the matching sheets. The bed was much more comfortable than sleeping on the floor in Madison's room. She was tired, but sleep eluded her. Thoughts of the last few days drifted in and out of her mind. Madison being spitting mad at her. Madison in pain. Jenny thanking her. Grayson grabbing hold of her little finger and hugging her tightly when they said their good-byes.

Madison had a wonderful support system here, and Ali was thankful for that. It was good to know that they would be here for her when Ali left. She lay in bed for what seemed like hours. She slipped out of bed and padded back down the hall to Madison's room. She leaned against the doorjamb and tried to convince herself that she was just checking on her. But her heart knew better. Her heart recognized the strong feelings of longing. Feelings that she had no idea what to do with.

CHAPTER TWELVE

Each day, Madison felt a little better. By the fourth day, she was still sore but could get up and down the stairs without assistance. Jenny informed them that she could cover a couple more days at the donut shop. It was time to tell Ali she could go home. Madison wasn't sure if Ali would be relieved or disappointed. She had really come through and had been a godsend.

Ali was already fixing breakfast as Madison, still moving slower than normal, made her way downstairs. The smell of bacon greeted her as she pushed open the swinging door to the kitchen. Ali was quietly singing, off tune. Her back was to Madison as she flipped pancakes at the stove. Madison stopped and just watched her for a couple of minutes. The last few days really opened her eyes to who Ali had become and who she still was. The fact that she was going to miss Ali surprised her. They had managed to cohabitate seamlessly.

Ali turned around and jumped. The spatula she was holding flew into the air and landed on the floor with a thud. She laughed, obviously embarrassed. "I didn't hear you come in. How long have you been standing there?"

"An hour and a half."

"Liar."

Simultaneously, they bent to pick up the spatula, and ended up face-to-face, inches apart. Madison's gaze landed on Ali's lips. Red. Full. Looking so kissable in that moment. It took her another second or two to get a handle on her feelings and that thought—that very unwise thought. She stood up a little too quicky and felt an unpleasant twinge in her back. "Ooh."

Ali was up and next to her in an instant. "I don't think you're quite ready for calisthenics yet. Here. Sit down." She took Madison by the elbow and eased her into a nearby kitchen chair.

"It was just a little glitch. I'm all right." Ali raised one eyebrow. "Seriously." She waved a hand toward the stove. "I think your food is burning."

"Oh shit." Ali moved with lightning speed, grabbed the handle of the frying pan, and moved it to the center of the stove. She flipped over a pancake and showed it to Madison. "Should still be good."

Madison stared down at the black pancake and tried to decide if Ali was joking. "Um. Yeah. It looks fine. You can have that one. I prefer mine a little less cooked."

"Oh, come on. This one's perfect." Ali laughed. "Luckily, this was the last one. I have a whole stack here." She threw the burnt one in the trash and picked up a plate full of fluffy pancakes. "I think we need to eat in the dining room. That smell is pretty bad."

"Agreed. What can I do to help?"

Ali turned the fan over the stove on. "Nothing. Go make yourself comfortable at the dining room table. I'll bring everything out."

"I'm not an invalid—anymore, anyway. I can help. In fact, why don't you go sit down and I'll serve you. You have waited on me enough. It's my turn."

"I'm thinking—"

"Don't start a sentence with a lie," Madison interrupted.

Ali laughed. She hadn't heard that line since—well, since the last time Madison had said it to her years ago. For a moment, she was transported back in time, to happier days. Much happier. "I'm thinking," she repeated. "That you shouldn't be pushing it, considering the back spasm you just had."

"You win. I'll go sit and let you wait on me hand and foot."

"Good. Go."

Madison padded over to the dining room through the open doorway. She was barely gone a minute when she called Ali.

Ali stopped what she was doing and went to see what Madison needed. "Is it pain? Do you need the heating pad?"

"No." Madison pointed at the wall. "There's a spider."

Ali remembered that Madison was not fond of insects. She laughed. "That little old thing. He's cute."

"He may be cute, but I don't want him in the house."

"I'll take care of it." Ali headed back to the kitchen to get a cup and a piece of cardboard or something to scoop him up with.

"Don't hurt him."

Ali stopped in her tracks. "What?"

"Don't hurt him. Can you just get something to move him outside?"

This wasn't the old Madison Ali remembered. She would have squashed that critter and not thought twice about it. "You used to hate spiders."

"I still do, but just because they freak me out doesn't give me the right to kill it. I'll move it outside if you don't want to."

Ali smiled. Madison's compassion had expanded to include spiders. Her heart swelled at the thought of it. "No. I'll do it. I agree. He should just be encouraged to go live somewhere else." Ali found an old paper Chinese food menu in a drawer. She placed a small glass over the spider, slid the menu between the glass and the wall, and captured the little guy. She shook him loose off the side of the deck outside.

"You and Jasper are now safe," Ali said when she returned.

"Jasper?"

"Yeah. That's what he said his name is. You don't think he was lying do you?"

"No. Not unless he's in the witness protection program, and as far as I know they don't usually include spiders in that."

"They do if the spider testified against a mob boss."

Madison laughed and Ali warmed to the sound of it. "You're such a smart-ass."

"Hey. I saved your life and you call me names."

Ali gathered the food and place settings and made several trips between the dining room and kitchen setting everything up.

"I feel like a slug sitting here watching you go back and forth and not helping," Madison said.

"You have a hard time relaxing, don't you?" Ali poured orange juice into Madison's glass.

"I can relax. It's just that I haven't done anything for days. I'm getting restless."

"Would you like to do something today? We could go to the ocean, sit on the beach. It's supposed to be a beautiful day."

"That's just more sitting. Unless you want to go." Madison poured syrup on her pancake and took a bite.

Ali racked her brains. What else was there to do in Clyde that wouldn't stress Madison's back? She came up empty. "Did you have anything in mind?"

"We can go to the ocean—"

"That's what I said," Ali interrupted.

"And take a stroll on the boardwalk. The exercise will do me good."

"Oh. I didn't know there was a boardwalk." Ali half expected Madison to blast her for not knowing stuff that had changed in the last twenty years. She didn't. Ali realized that Madison hadn't done that since her back went out. Maybe she wasn't quite as mad at Ali because she was helping her. Or maybe she wasn't as mad because she realized Ali wasn't her enemy. Whatever caused the change, Ali was glad.

"You don't think that will be too much for you? Remember it's an hour's drive."

"I can put the seat back so I'm reclining on the ride. We can walk some, and if it gets to be too much we can sit on the beach for a bit. I have beach chairs in the garage."

"If you're sure," Ali said. The last thing she wanted was for Madison to be in more pain.

"I'm sorry. I should have asked you if you mind driving that far." Ali would drive a hundred miles if it meant spending more time with Madison. "It's no problem. I'm the one who suggested it in the first place."

Madison laughed. "Oh yeah. That's where I heard it. I'll give you gas money."

"Stop being ridiculous. I'll buy the gas—but I'm going to make you pump it." Ali dived into her breakfast.

"Okay."

"I'm just kidding. You are going to take it as easy as you can. I may even carry you on the boardwalk."

"Good plan. Then I can take care of you for a week when your back goes out."

"Deal."

They finished their meal, Ali cleaned up and Madison located the beach chairs. They packed a few things, sunscreen, water bottles and such.

Madison adjusted the car seat and was fast asleep before they had driven twenty minutes. Ali attributed it to days of being in pain. That could wear you out for sure. That gave Ali time to think. Maybe too much time. She knew the dreaded conversation was just around the corner. Madison was getting better every day, and soon Ali's services would no longer be needed. She would have no excuse to stay and Madison would expect her to go home. She didn't want to go.

Besides not wanting to leave Madison, she was starting to appreciate small town life again. It was the simple things, like going into a smaller grocery store and not have it mobbed with people. And folks you didn't even know said hello or at least nodded to you, acknowledging your existence. It felt nice. It wasn't that Syracuse was a bad place to live. Ali had gotten along just fine there. It was just that more people meant more separation. She had been back in Clyde for less than two weeks but settled back in as if she never left. But she had left. And she had to leave again. She just didn't want it to be too soon. She and Madison had gotten on well the last several days. She still longed for the possibility of them getting back together. She played out the scenario in her mind.

Madison could cut her hours at O's if she wanted to. With the money Ali made they could afford to do that. Madison would go to work, Ali would write, then make dinner for the two of them. A white tablecloth covered the dining room table, two candles in the center. The table set for two and dinner staying warm until Madison walked through the door. Ali would greet her with a lingering kiss. It was stupid. It was never going to happen. Stop wanting what you can never have.

"What are you thinking?" Madison asked.

Ali hadn't notice that she had woken up, and the question startled her. Good question. Probably best not to answer it. "Nothing."

"You do realize I can see right through you, don't you?"

She always could. Apparently, not everything had changed in twenty years. "Then what am I thinking?"

Madison took a few moments to answer. "You're thinking that I'm getting pretty self-reliant and you will be going home soon. What I don't know is what your thoughts are on that subject."

"So, your mind reading skills only go so far?"

Madison put her seat back up into an upright position. "Ali, let's be serious here for a moment. Can you tell me how you feel about that? Please?"

Ali rolled the question around in her mind. She knew without a doubt how she felt. What she didn't know was how much of it to admit to Madison. Madison had made it clear that she wanted Ali gone, but that was before she hurt her back. They hadn't discussed it since then, and she had no idea how Madison felt now. "How do you feel about it?" she asked, bracing herself for the answer.

"Oh no. You aren't turning this back on me. I asked you. I want you to tell me honestly how you feel."

Honestly? Okay, she could do that. "I've gotten used to being back in Clyde." Okay, so that was only partially honest.

"And?" Obviously, Madison wasn't going to let her get away with that answer.

"And—I would like to stay longer. I'm not really ready to go home." There it was, out in the open. Best to leave out the part that she wanted them to get back together.

"Don't you want to get back to your life there? Your friends? Your goldfish, I don't know. Whatever?"

Ali laughed. "Goldfish?"

Madison laughed along. "I don't know. I just always pictured you with a goldfish. I just didn't like the thought of you being alone and I didn't want to imagine you with anyone else."

"You thought of me?"

"Ali, how could I not. You may have disappeared from my life, but you didn't disappear from my heart. I mean. It took a while. But… I mean…" Madison seemed to be stumbling over her words.

"Am I still in your heart?" Ali asked, not sure she wanted to hear the answer.

Madison took so long to answer that Ali was sure she wasn't going to. Her face flushed with heat as she waited. She hoped she wasn't turning red.

"I'm going to try to answer as honestly as I can. I think you deserve that." Another long pause. "A piece of my heart will always belong to you. You were my first love. How could I forget that?" Pause. "That being said, you also shattered that same heart into pieces. That's not something you get over easily."

There it was. Not the answer she was hoping for, but not as bad as it could have been. "I know. Believe me, I know the feeling because I had a broken heart too. Granted it was of my own doing, but I didn't know that for a whole lot of years. But for me I got over the broken heart as soon as I saw you."

"As soon as you saw me? I doubt that. You certainly didn't act like you were over it."

"Maybe as soon as I realized that I had been the one in the wrong. I wanted to make it up to you as soon as I found out the truth."

"You've made up for it these past several days. I want you to know I forgive you for leaving, and I'm sorry I was such a bitch when you first showed up."

Ali couldn't stop smiling. Madison forgave her. She still needed to work on forgiving herself, but Madison forgave her. That was more important. "I don't blame you for not being the most welcoming when I appeared out of the blue."

Madison knew that Ali wanted more than an apology, she wanted another chance. Madison wasn't ready to give her that. But she also didn't have to send her away so soon. "You said you aren't ready to go home yet. Why don't you stay around a while longer? I'm sure there are other people, old friends from school, that you would like to see."

"There's no one here I kept in touch with. When I left, I left nothing here to come back to. My parents moved to Florida right after I graduated so I didn't have to come back here for them. But I really would like to stay longer, if you don't mind. I mean we had a deal."

"That was a stupid deal anyway. I had no right to demand that you leave town. Tell you what, as soon as I take my last dose of medicine we can go out for another drink—or two—or four, and I won't make you go home the next day."

There was that smile again. "Deal."

"Good. There's a bar three blocks from my house. We can go there and walk home and not have to worry about driving."

"There's a gay bar so close?"

The look of surprise on Ali's face was endearing. "No. It's a straight bar. It's still Clyde you know. The town is not quite ready for that. But the good news is they don't ask your sexual orientation at the door."

"Smart-ass."

"Thank you. I knew my ass was nice, I didn't know it was smart as well."

"You do have a nice ass. Remember you still need to baby your back. Now is not the time to start to overdo it. Besides, I want you off your meds so we can go to that straight bar. I'll have to practice my straight walk, though, so I can pass."

"You have a straight walk that's different than your regular walk, which I assume is your gay walk?"

"I do. I'll show you when we get to the boardwalk."

"I can hardly wait."

"You are going to be sooo impressed."

"Turn left up here. Ignore the signs. I know a shortcut."

Ali followed Madison's directions. They led her to a back parking lot behind the boardwalk. "How did you know about this lot? It's not for the general public."

"Nope. It's not. But it's much closer to the boardwalk. My dad used to set up a small donut stand here in the summer. Jen and I would run it for him."

Ali turned the car off and turned to Madison. "You must miss him—and your mom. They were always so kind to me."

"I do. It wasn't easy, that's for sure. But Jenny and I have each other, so that helps a lot. I hope you keep in touch with your parents. Because once they're gone it changes everything."

"I do. I usually talk to them once a week. I guess I'm a little behind. I haven't called them since I've been back in Clyde."

"Ali."

Ali held up her hand. "I know. I know. I'll call them later."

"Give them my best, please. I always liked your parents."

"They adored you." Ali paused. "I'm so sorry, Madison."

"Sorry for what?"

"About your parents."

Madison shrugged. "Thanks. I haven't been back here since Dad died."

"You okay doing this?"

"Absolutely. I've just been too busy with O's to make the time. It's good to be back." She was looking forward to showing Ali around. "Ready?"

"Yep." Ali got out of the car and went around to Madison's side. She offered Madison her hand. Madison appreciated the help. Her back wasn't a hundred percent yet, and Ali was right. She needed to take it easy.

"Remember to let me know if you need to rest or if you have pain. Did you remember your pills?"

Madison patted her pocket. "Want to see my straight walk now? I've been dying to show you." Ali didn't wait for an answer. She took several steps, swinging her hips wide from side to side.

"Oh, Ali, please do not do that when we go out."

Ali turned her face to Madison. "You're just jealous." She turned around and pranced in a circle ending up back by Madison's side. She slipped her arm through Madison's. It felt familiar and nice. Madison fought the comfortable feeling. She considered pulling her arm away, but having Ali supporting her while they walked helped. A lot. "This okay?" Ali asked as if reading her mind. "I thought it might help."

"It does. It's fine."

They cut between two booths and stepped onto the boardwalk. There were a few more booths than the last time Madison had been here. One side of the boardwalk was lined with various venders, most of which were closed and probably wouldn't open for another couple of weeks. The other side was opened to the beach. Madison took a deep breath and filled her lungs with the fresh salt air. She hadn't realized how much she'd missed that smell. The sound of the waves crashing on the shore were far enough away that they were soothing but not overwhelming.

"Cotton candy," Ali said.

"What?"

Ali pointed up ahead. "Cotton candy. I love cotton candy. I hope they have yellow."

Yes. Madison remembered. They were seventeen when they borrowed Ali's dad's car and drove to the Maryland State Fair, less than thirty minutes away. Their parents probably wouldn't have let them go by themselves if it had been any farther. Ali had downed a large bag of yellow cotton candy almost single-handedly and bought another two bags to take home. She always did have a sweet tooth. Madison could taste the sugary sweetness on her lips when they had a major make-out session later in the car before driving home. The memory made Madison smile.

"Do you mind if I get some?" Ali asked her.

Madison let go of Ali's arm and pulled a twenty-dollar bill from her pocket. "Can we get a small bag of yellow cotton candy?" she asked the man behind the counter. "And if I pay for two large bags, can you set it aside until we're ready to leave?"

"Sure."

Madison paid the man, got her change, and handed the bag to Ali. Ali's face lit up with a smile. Madison saw that same smile on seventeen-year-old Ali so many years ago. It was one of the things that made Madison fall in love with her.

"Thank you. You didn't have to do that."

"I couldn't have you drooling all over the boardwalk."

Ali pulled a small chunk of cotton candy out of the bag and held it up to Madison.

Madison let Ali feed it to her. It tasted just like she remembered Ali's lips tasting. She shook away the memory. She just wanted to enjoy today. Taking a walk down memory lane was not part of her plans.

Ali ate several pieces and offered another to Madison. Madison shook her head.

"That's right. I remember. You aren't much into sweets. Ironic that you own a donut shop."

"Ironic that you're a writer and you…"

Ali stopped walking. "And I what?"

"And you are with someone who can't think of anything ironic about that."

"Goof." They continued at a slow pace.

"Ali, I'm glad you got your dream of being a writer."

"Thank you. Sometimes I think I suck at it."

Madison was surprised. Ali seemed so sure of herself and what she wanted. "Why do you say that?"

"Because I sit down to write a book and my brain tells me I don't know what I'm doing."

"You said you're successful, so obviously your brain is an idiot."

Ali laughed. "I try to prove my brain wrong. I start a book flying by the seat of my pants, making it up as I go. I get about halfway done and my brain starts again, telling me that the book sucks."

"How do you keep going?" Madison found it fascinating that that was Ali's writing process.

"I try to remember that I go through the same thing with every book and they seem to come out okay. I get decent reviews."

"I'll bet they're more than decent. I'll bet they're glowing."

"I'll have to read some of the bad ones to you sometime."

"How do you deal with that?" Madison wasn't sure she could handle writing a book, sending it out in the world and having people say bad things about it. She was much too sensitive for that.

"First, I take an honest look at it and see if they have a valid point. I'm always trying to improve. Then I usually laugh."

That didn't make any sense. "Laugh?"

"Yeah. If I can't laugh at someone else's opinion of my work, then it's time to quit. You learn to develop a thick skin."

There weren't a lot of people out on the boardwalk on a weekday. Madison was glad of that. They could take their time and not be dodging anyone. Her back probably couldn't handle that. "I would cry."

"You always were the sensitive type."

"And sometimes you tried to be too strong and independent. You tried to handle so much on your own." Madison didn't say it with any rancor but regretted the words as soon as she said them.

"And look where that's gotten me. Alone."

"I'm sorry, Ali."

"For what? For saying the truth?" Ali tied the bag of cotton candy closed. She'd barely eaten any of it. "I never have been good at accepting help. I'm trying not to be like that anymore. I'm learning that I don't have to do everything by myself. I can rely on other people. I let you buy me cotton candy, didn't I?" She flashed Madison one of those full toothed grins.

Madison refused to let it into her heart, even though it was trying to beat its way in. The twinge in her back was almost a welcomed distraction. "How about we get something a little more substantial to eat. I'm going to need a pill soon."

"Of course. It looks like there's a burger stand ahead. Will that do?"

Madison nodded. She took hold of Ali's arm again.

She took a pill as soon as she took a couple of bites of her burger. She only had a couple more days of medicine left. As long as she didn't overdo it, that should be enough. Then she would have a drink with Ali as promised. A drink as friends. A drink to show Ali how much she appreciated all her help.

She had had no right to tell Ali when she had to leave town. That just wasn't right. To her surprise, she was actually looking forward to spending more time with her when she wasn't in such serious pain. She had told Ali she could stay, but they hadn't discussed where Ali would stay. She thought about it as she munched on her burger and fries. Should she continue to let Ali stay with her or suggest that she go back to the hotel? There was no reason she couldn't stay with Madison in the guest room. It had worked out so far. Besides Ali turned out to be a great cook and Madison wouldn't mind eating a few more of her meals— and having another drink with her—and having her around for a little longer.

"I think we should take it easy," Ali said after she threw their food wrappers away. "I'm not used to all this walking." Madison knew she said that to get her to rest. She was sure Ali could walk a mile or two with no problem.

"Should we sit on the beach with our toes in the sand or would you prefer to head home?"

"Sand between my toes sounds nice."

"Tell you what, you sit on that bench over there." Ali pointed to a spot just off the boardwalk. "And I'll go get the beach chairs from the car."

"I'm not an invalid. I can go with you."

"Madison, please sit."

"I thought you said you weren't going to try to do everything by yourself anymore."

Ali shook her head. "Are you sure?"

"Yep. I'm not going to push it. I'll hold onto your arm. We'll go slow, get the chairs, and sit by the water. I'm fine."

"Okay." She put her arm—bent at the elbow—out to Madison. Madison took it and they started back toward the car. Her back was a little sore, but no real pain. She hadn't had another twinge since taking her medicine.

They got the chairs and settled down by the water. Madison slipped off her shoes and Ali did the same. The sand was warm against the bottom of her feet but felt considerably cooler when she dug them in. She wiggled her toes digging in deeper. They relaxed into a comfortable silence. Madison leaned back, closed her eyes, and lifted her chin to get the full effect of the warm sun on her face.

Her mind drifted back to another time. A younger time. Fragmented memories floated through. Ali in her two-piece bathing suit running through the sand toward Madison, her head tilted back laughing. Grabbing Madison around the waist trying to pull her into the cool water. Falling together in the surf, getting water up her nose, and laughing until she couldn't breathe. Ali's parents telling them it was time to leave and holding Ali's hand hidden under a towel in the back seat on the ride back home. She was so in love with her.

At times she had to work hard not to let it show. They had to hide it away from the world. It was both maddening and exciting to have a secret that was only between the two of them. She stopped her floating memories before they got to the painful part. The part where Ali left, and Madison thought she would dry up like an old leaf and just crumble in the wind. Today she just wanted to think about the good things. Ali would be staying longer. And she was looking forward to it, although she wasn't ready to admit that yet—to Ali—or to herself.

CHAPTER THIRTEEN

Madison's back was pretty much back to normal. She finished her pills, although she said she probably didn't need the last few. Ali convinced her to take them, not because she was a fan of taking unnecessary medicine, but because she wanted to make sure Madison didn't have any more pain.

Ali wished she had brought some nicer clothes with her. She hadn't packed for a long stay, and it was obvious as she thumbed through what she had hanging in the closet in Madison's guest room. Not only had Madison invited her to stay in town longer, she said she could still stay at her house. Ali was more than pleasantly surprised. Her maroon shirt with a bit of sheen to it would have to do. It was cut lower than Ali usually wore, but the color looked good on her and it would pair nice with her good jeans.

If she was home, she would pair this outfit with a simple gold chain around her neck and her favorite hoop earrings. But she was out of luck. She studied herself in the full-length mirror on the back of the guest room door. She looked good enough. After all, this wasn't a date. It was two friends having drinks. Would Madison consider them friends? Probably. She certainly acted like they were friends. Ali knew she needed to put aside any hopes of them getting back together. She could settle for being friends. Reluctantly.

"Are you almost ready?" Madison called up the stairs.

"Yep. Coming." Ali buttoned the cuffs on her shirt, grabbed a light sweater, and headed down the stairs.

"You look nice," Madison said.

"Thanks. You do too." Madison sported a black long-sleeve shirt with thin pinstripes and gray slacks. Her long dark hair had extra curls and her dark lashes were enhanced with just enough mascara to bring out the sparkle in her brown eyes. Unlike Ali's, her outfit was enhanced with a silver pendant on a thin chain and silver studs in her ears. Her beauty was on full display, and Ali felt underdressed in comparison.

"I have a necklace that would look great with that shirt if you want to borrow it."

"I would really appreciate that."

Madison ran upstairs, proof of how much better her back was, and came down holding a gold chain with a ruby dangling gently from it. "Turn around," she said.

Ali did as she was told. She closed her eyes and tried to ignore the rush that went through her as Madison brushed her hair to one side and slipped the chain around her neck and set the clasp. "There. What do you think?"

Ali took a couple of steps toward the mirror by the front door. She caught a glimpse of Madison behind her. "Beautiful," she said, forgetting to look at the necklace.

"Let's get going. I've been sitting on that couch too long. I need to get back out in the world."

They walked side by side, Ali careful to keep a reasonable amount of distance between them the few blocks to Rosie's Bar. If memory served, there used to be a flower shop where the bar now stood. Ali held the door open for Madison and followed her in. It took a few minutes for her eyes to adjust to the dim lighting. The place was sparsely populated, and Ali assumed it was because it was still early. A few guys were setting up a drum set, microphones, and various paraphernalia in one corner.

"This place will be mobbed soon," Madison said. "Let's sit over there." She indicated a table farthest away from the band. "It'll be quieter and easier to talk without shouting."

Ali followed Madison to the table. The server took only a few minutes to arrive, order pad in hand. "What can I get you gals?" she asked. She had a wad of gum shoved in her cheek that she didn't attempt to hide.

"Whiskey sour," Madison said. "Beer?" she asked Ali.

"I think I'll have something a little more exotic tonight. Can I have a margarita, please?"

"Ooh, that is exotic," Madison teased her.

A margarita seemed fitting seeing that was what she was drinking when Ali bravely—maybe more like foolishly—sent the letters to her exes, bringing her here to this moment. This moment with Madison, a place she never thought she would be.

Three drinks later, Madison reached across the small table and ran a single finger over the ruby dangling from the gold chain a few inches above Ali's cleavage. "That does look nice on you."

The unexpected contact sent a surge of electricity through Ali that landed squarely in her crotch. Whoa. It had been a long time since a simple touch had had such an effect on her. She searched her memory to see if any lovers since Madison had had the ability to do that—turn her on with a single touch. The answer was a resounding no.

Madison pulled her hand back almost as suddenly as she had reached out to touch the necklace. What was she thinking touching Ali like that? She could only blame it on the alcohol—and the fact that Ali looked so sexy with her low-cut blouse exposing so much of her skin, the tops of her breasts peeking out. Madison remembered what it was like to run a tongue over that skin. The memory made her wet. She pushed the urge to do that now away. Not only was that a bad idea, but to do it in a bar—a straight bar—made the thought totally outrageous. The last thing she wanted to do was lead Ali on, and that move would surely have done just that. She laughed out loud at how stupid her brain—and her libido—were being. She felt like a teenage boy getting his first glimpse of boobs and letting his hormones go crazy.

She had barely brushed Ali's skin, but the feeling left her wanting. Wanting what? Wanting sex? It had been quite a while. Wanting Ali? That was just a bad idea. Wanting a connection. Ali just happened to be the one who was close by, she reasoned.

"Thanks," Ali said.

"Thanks for what?" Madison had been so lost in her head that she lost the thread of their conversation."

"You said your necklace looks good on me. Thanks for letting me borrow it. Thanks for the compliment. Just thanks."

Madison had to laugh at herself. "I did say that didn't I?" She drained the last swallow of her drink and waved the server over. "I think I'm going to have another. How about you?" she asked Ali.

The server arrived before Ali had a chance to answer. "Another round." Madison read her name tag. "Linda. Please."

"Can I just get a glass of water?" Ali added.

"Bring her water and another margarita." She brought her attention to Ali. "I hate to drink alone."

Linda waited, her attention on Ali.

"That's fine," Ali said. "And bring a glass of water for my friend here too."

Friend. It seemed wrong for Ali to refer to her as friend. They had been so much more than that once. They weren't lovers anymore so that didn't fit. Girlfriends? No, they certainly weren't that. But friends didn't seem quite right. Acquaintances was far too casual a word considering what they had once meant to each other. Too much thinking and not enough drinking. Another drink would dull her mind and help stop the train of thoughts that were invading her good time.

"Where'd you go?"

"What?"

"You were somewhere in your head for a bit. What were you thinking?"

"That I'm glad we can sit here together and have a drink." Close enough to the truth. "Or four."

Madison giggled. What? I don't giggle. Must be the alcohol. Maybe I should slow down. Linda arrived with their drinks as if on cue. Madison took a long sip. It went down easy. Maybe too easy.

"Water might be a good idea before you down that," Ali pointed out gently.

Madison took another long sip before grabbing her glass of water. "Yes, Mother." She giggled again. Damn. If Ali minded the comment, she didn't show it.

Madison finished the water in record time and returned to her drink. She was already over her self-imposed three-drink limit. She wasn't sure why and she didn't feel like analyzing it. She had done enough analyzing for tonight. "Tell me about your life in Syracuse. Do you like it there?"

Ali sipped her water. "It's okay. You know how it only takes a little snow to close things down here?"

"Yeah."

"It takes a couple of feet there before anything shuts down."

"That's interesting, but I want to know about your life, not the weather." They really hadn't spent much time learning about each other's lives over the past week. That was probably Madison's fault. She really hadn't cared to know too much about Ali and even more, she didn't want Ali to know about her life. Not that she had anything to hide.

"Okay. Let's see. We've already established that I don't have a goldfish."

Giggle. Stop it!

Ali smiled. She seemed to be enjoying Madison and her foolish laugh. "I don't have much of a social life. Writing is pretty solitary and doesn't offer much of an opportunity to make friends."

"That makes me sad."

"It's not that I don't have any friends. I have a very good friend, Charley, that I'm close too."

The sadness was pushed out by jealousy. Oh my God, Madison, stop it. This needs to be your last drink because obviously you've lost your mind. "And is Charley a boy or girl?" She was well aware of the fact that she sounded like she was in middle school.

"Interesting question."

"Why? Are there other choices?"

"Actually, there are. Charley was born male but has a female side too."

"Left or right?"

"What?"

Madison plowed on with her silly question, despite the fact that her head was starting to spin. Or was it the room? "Is his female side on the left or right?"

"Top."

"Oh shit. I didn't even think of that." Madison laughed. "I'm sorry. I think I'm a little tipsy. I really do want to hear about Charley—and your life. Is he gender fluid?"

"Yeah. Sometimes he presents as male, but more often as female. We went to college together."

"You went in Syracuse, right? Your mother told me that much. But that was it."

"Madison, I'm so sorry about that."

"Stop apologizing. I already forgave you. Ali, I'm not happy with the way things turned out, but we can't undo it. We can just move forward. Now—Syracuse? That had been your original plan if I recall." She recalled a lot. There wasn't much about her time with Ali that she didn't remember. It had been the best time in her life—until it wasn't.

"Yes. Syracuse University. I stayed when I graduated. I did a lot of odd jobs until my writing took off."

"I'm so proud of you. You made it. You did what you set out to do."

Ali shook her head. "I may have done all right with my career, and I'm very grateful for Charley, but the rest of my life is a mess."

Madison found that hard to believe. Ali seemed so put together. "How so?"

Ali finished her water and took a sip of her fourth drink. "You don't want to hear about my pathetic life." She raised her hand to get the server's attention.

"Yes, I do."

Linda was there in a flash. "Can we get a pepperoni pizza and an order of cheese sticks?" She turned to Madison. "Is there anything else you'd like?"

Madison hadn't even thought about eating. They'd had an early dinner and her stomach growled at the mention of food. "Let's get the homemade potato chips. They are to die for."

"Sounds good. And more water, please."

Linda wrote the order on her pad and disappeared into the crowd of people that had gathered without Madison's awareness.

"So?" Madison sensed Ali's reluctance to talk about her life and wondered if she should let it go.

"You know that letter I sent you?"

Madison nodded.

"Charley suggested that I write to my exes because I had somehow messed up relationship after relationship. He thought maybe I could gain some insight as to why."

"I have a confession," Madison said. "I didn't read past the first part."

"And then you threw it in the trash can and kicked the can, I'm guessing?"

"Something like that."

"I don't blame you. I had no idea I had hurt you. I would have set it on fire if I had been in your position."

"Did you get responses from your other exes?" Other exes. Madison didn't like the thought of Ali being hurt in other relationships—or even having other relationships.

"I did. I realized that I was never invested. The companionship was nice, but I never really connected with anyone."

That didn't seem like the Ali she knew. "Did you figure out why?"

Linda reappeared with a basket of thick, light brown potato chips, two small plates, and a bottle of ketchup. "Pizza and bread sticks will be out in a bit." She poured water into each of their glasses.

"Partially. I have more thinking to do on it."

"What have you figured out so far?"

"I didn't figure it out until I came back here and saw you. It was just reinforced once I knew that you hadn't cheated on me," Ali said once the waitress left.

Madison was pretty sure she knew where Ali was going with this and considered stopping her. But she was the one who had asked the question, and to stop her now just seemed cruel.

Ali knew she shouldn't reveal too much, but Madison had asked. She owed her the truth. "I had never gotten over you. Not totally anyway." There it was. It was out. She studied Madison for her reaction. Whatever she was thinking, it wasn't written on her face. Asking her outright seemed out of the question. Time for a change of subject. "When did you take over the donut shop? And who changed the name?" If Madison minded the sudden change of subject, she didn't object.

Madison gave Ali the details, the storm that ruined the original sign, the new name, her dad dying and Madison and

Jenny stepping up to run the place and losing her mother two years later. "I run the day-to-day stuff and Jenny handles the business end. If you recall, math was not my strong suit in school."

Ali laughed. "I remember sneaking you the answers to math tests stuck in a gum wrapper. I think that's what made you fall in love with me." Uh oh. She wasn't sure if she had overstepped. Madison more than likely didn't want to be reminded of when they were together, not after what Ali did to her.

"There were so many more reasons than some test answers that made me fall in love with you," Madison said.

Ali felt herself flush with heat as she stared into Madison's brown eyes and Madison stared back. The eye contact felt so intense. Almost too intense. She wanted so badly to kiss her. She leaned forward but stopped herself in time. Madison, however, continued the movement Ali had started until their lips met. The kiss lingered for what seemed like an eternity but was only a few moments. Ali wasn't sure which one of them broke the contact, but it was over as quickly as it had begun.

Oh shit, Madison thought. *Did I really just do that? Damn alcohol.* No. It wasn't the alcohol. Not totally anyway. It was how hot sexy Ali looked with her low-cut shirt and just enough makeup to make her skin glow. It was the memories of loving her in high school and everything they had shared. It was a connection she, like Ali, hadn't truly felt with anyone else. Her lips tingled from the contact.

"Umm. Pizza and breadsticks."

Madison turned her head and looked up at Linda, balancing a pan of pizza in one hand and a basket of breadsticks in the other, a flustered look on her face.

Ali moved the basket of potato chips, which they hadn't touched, to the side and Linda set the rest of the food down. "Can I get you anything else?"

"I don't think so," Madison said. "Ali?"

"Huh? Um, what?" She was obviously flustered by the kiss.

"Do you need anything else?"

"Ah, no. Thanks."

Linda pulled a handful of napkins from the pocket on her apron and set them on the table. She left without another word. Seemed that kiss knocked everyone out of kilter. The thing was Madison didn't regret it. She knew she should. She knew it couldn't happen again, but for a few short seconds, she was back in high school and she was kissing the person she loved. It happened. It was over. Madison didn't plan on talking about it. She hoped Ali didn't either.

Ali silently pulled a slice of pizza from the pan, put it on a plate, and set it in front of Madison. She took another slice and took a large bite, chewing slowly, almost thoughtfully. "Sooo," Madison let the word linger. "My sister, Jenny, was never much for working at the donut shop when we were kids. Oh sure, she would stop in to get donuts to eat…"

Ali was still silently chewing the same bite.

"Ali?"

"Yes?" At least she brought her eyes up to Madison this time.

"Nothing. I was just talking about the donut shop."

"I always loved hanging out there after school." And just like that, Ali was back. "Your dad was always so nice to me. I often wondered if he would be as nice if he knew we were more than friends."

"I did tell them you know. About us."

Ali seemed surprised. "You did?"

"Yes. It was a few months after you left. They said it didn't change anything. They cared about you. Of course, they weren't happy about the way you left without a word." Madison regretted saying it as soon as it came out of her mouth.

"I'm sor—"

Madison put up her hand.

"Sorry about saying sorry."

Madison laughed. "I accept your apology for apologizing."

Ali laughed too. Madison was relieved. Guess she hadn't shocked Ali too bad with that kiss. She just wanted to get back on track with her. Keep it light. Madison took a bite of her pizza. "Mm. This is good."

"Do you come here a lot?" Ali asked between bites.

"No. I almost never go to bars." Unless I am meeting a date from online. And then it was usually the gay bar at the edge of town.

"Why? This is so close to your house."

"My alcohol consumption is usually limited to wine at Jenny's. I don't know. I don't go out much."

"I asked you before if you had someone special in your life. You wouldn't answer me, but I assume you don't, or she would have been the one taking care of you, instead of me."

Madison had no problem answering that question now. There was no sense keeping it from Ali. "You would be correct. There is no one special currently."

"But there has been?"

Madison drained the last of her drink, briefly considered ordering another one, but decided against it. God only knew what would happen if she had even more alcohol coursing through her. That kiss might have been just the tip of the iceberg if she were drunker. She was suddenly aware that she hadn't answered Ali's question. "Of course. I briefly considered becoming a nun when you left, but the celibate life didn't seem that appealing. That and the fact that I'm not Catholic."

"How come it didn't work out? Any relationship."

"They just didn't." Ali got the sense that Madison didn't want to talk about it. Maybe she didn't really know why none of them worked out, just like Ali hadn't known—until she did. Or maybe she figured it was none of Ali's business. Maybe it was none of Ali's business why Madison had kissed her and then pretended like it didn't happen. But it did happen. And it was electric. She felt more in those three seconds than she had having full-on sex with her last few partners. How was that even possible? It wasn't. Surely, she must have imagined it. No kiss could have that much power. She was having trouble wrapping her head around it. Maybe another drink would help.

Ali stared at her empty glass as if the answers she was seeking were hiding there. The extra drink hadn't helped like she hoped. Maybe that was because she wasn't even sure of the questions.

"Are you ready to go?" Madison asked her.

"Yep. Should we have this food boxed up to take home?" Ali asked. They had barely touched any of it.

"Sure. This is my treat by the way."

"No. You are not paying for this. That's just crazy. It's on me."

"You took such good care of me. This doesn't even start to repay you. It's the least I could do."

"Do you always do the least you can do?" Ali teased her.

"You are just so funny, aren't you?"

"I think so."

"That makes one of us." Madison waved the server over, handed her her credit card before Ali had a chance to object, and asked for a take home box.

The night air was cool, and Ali was glad she had decided to bring a sweater. They were only a few yards from the bar when Ali stumbled. There was a dip in the sidewalk, she was sure. Consuming so much alcohol had nothing to do with it. At least that's what she told herself. "Whoa." Madison grabbed her arm, stopping her from face-planting on the sidewalk. She linked her arm through Ali's as soon as she was upright again.

"I'm not drunk, you know. You don't have to hold me up."

"Well, I am. I was hoping you would hold me up."

"It would be my pleasure." Ali smiled in the dark.

"Doesn't take much to give you pleasure," Madison said.

The words sent a shiver through Ali. "Oh, if you only knew what gives me pleasure."

Loaded words. Madison wasn't sure she should respond. She remembered a great deal that would have given Ali pleasure twenty years ago. But they were girls then. She silently wondered what it would take to give Ali, the woman, pleasure now. There was a small piece of her that wanted to find out. Maybe more than a small piece. But that wouldn't be fair to Ali. It would only lead her on and end up in more heartbreak for her. Besides, they were both drunk. Drunken sex, while it would probably be great, would just be stupid.

"Thank you," Ali said.

"For what?"

"Everything. Tonight. Allowing me back in your life. Forgiving me."

"Thank you back. For all your help. For being the same kind, giving Ali that I used to know." She left out the word loving, although she thought it. "I had a nice time tonight."

They got back to her house much too soon. Once inside, she knew they would go their separate ways, she would go to her room and Ali would go down the hall to the guest room. Just feet away but it felt like it was a million miles. Madison felt close to Ali tonight. A feeling she thought she could never have with her again. It was surprising. And somewhat alarming.

CHAPTER FOURTEEN

B aby girl, it sounds like things are going well," Charley said. "Where do you go from here?"

Ali pulled her feet up under her on the couch. It was Madison's first day back at the donut shop. Ali planned on helping her with the lunchtime crowd. Her back seemed to be fine, but Ali didn't want her to overdo it.

"I'm going to stick around a few more days, just to make sure Madison doesn't need any more help. Then I guess I'm coming home."

"I will be very glad to have you back. I've had to drink all by myself, and damn, it gets so lonely without you. I need you more than Madison Parker does."

"Thanks for the guilt trip, Charley."

"You're welcome, sugarplum."

"I've just got so many mixed feelings. I didn't expect to feel so drawn in. All I want is to be close to Madison and it kills me to know I can't."

"Tell me about this kiss Madison Parker laid on you."

"There's not much to tell. Her lips were so soft. Softer than I remember. Her breath smelled like whiskey, but sweeter somehow. There was the slightest flicker of her tongue. So light it was barely there, but the feeling…" Ali paused trying to come up with the right words. "The feeling went throughout my whole body. It just doesn't make sense."

"That was a whole lot of words for not much to tell. Ali, that sounds like love. Or at least lust."

Ali made her way into the kitchen and put the tea kettle on to boil. "I have to admit so many of my feelings for her are back. I just don't know what to do with them."

"Why do you think she kissed you?"

"Too much to drink. Plain and simple. I don't think it meant anything to her. She didn't even mention it after it happened. I'm not even sure she remembered it. I got the impression that she doesn't usually drink that much."

"They say alcohol brings out the truth."

"They also say that alcohol makes you do things you wouldn't ordinarily do."

The tea kettle began its sharp whistle, and Ali removed it from the heat before it got too hot. She gathered what she needed and plopped a chai tea bag into a cup and poured hot water over it. "I don't believe I've ever heard *they* say that."

"You know everything they say?" Ali dunked the tea bag up and down several times.

"Pretty much."

"Good to know."

After she finished her tea, Ali set to making lunch. She wanted to surprise Madison with it. She hoped it would make her smile. There wasn't much she wouldn't do to see that smile.

"Good to have you back," Tom said to Madison.

"We really missed you," Joe added. "Your sister's nice, but she just isn't you. Glad you're feeling better."

It was good to be back, especially with her regulars, whom she considered friends. "Thank you. I missed you two as well."

"What ever happened with your ex-girlfriend? You seemed pretty peeved, pardon my French, when she showed up here. I hope you don't mind me asking," Tom said.

"You gave me good advice when you said I should hear her out. We've cleared up a few things." And got close again, she thought but didn't add. She didn't want to be answering any questions about her feelings toward Ali. "In fact, she helped me when I threw my back out. She's still in town but should be going back home soon."

Madison wasn't looking forward to that day. She liked having her around. A lot. More than she thought she should. The morning went by quickly, and Madison was relieved that she didn't have any back pain or even twitches, especially since she'd spent most of that time on her feet. She made herself a sandwich in the shop's kitchen and sat at her desk to eat a quick lunch. A knock on the door made her look up.

"I brought you lunch." Ali held up a paper bag. "I wasn't sure what you had here to eat. I mean I know you serve lunch here but didn't know if you would want something else. I see you have a sandwich. I can just put this in the fridge if you don't want it."

Madison's mood, which was good to begin with, went up a couple more notches. "I just made myself a turkey and Swiss sandwich. Can you beat that?"

"Does lobster, baked potato, and cheesy biscuit beat it?"

"Oh my God, yes. Are you serious?"

"Hell no. That would be way too much work."

"I'm not worth all that work? Thanks a lot."

Ali moved a pile of papers to the side of Madison's desk and set the bag down. "You are, but I thought comfort food was called for on your first day back at work. I made lasagna, with lots of extra sauce, just the way you like it. Let's see…" Ali peered into the bag. "And meatballs."

"Why are you so good to me?" Madison wouldn't have blamed Ali if she had left her stuck in her car when her back went out after the way Madison had treated her.

"'Cause, I like you a little bit." Ali held up her thumb and index finger about an inch apart. "Maybe even a little bit more than a little bit."

"Thank you. I like you a little bit more than a little bit too." Maybe a whole lot more than a little bit. "I hope you brought enough for both of us."

"I did. Okay if I go grab some plates and silverware from the kitchen?"

"Absolutely."

When Madison finished the last bite on her plate, she sat back and patted her stomach. "That was excellent. Thank you so much."

"No problem. I'm here to work. What do you want me to do?"

"Want to make the donuts?" Madison laughed at the face Ali made. "Just kidding. You can take orders. Valerie will show you how to run the register. I need to catch up on some paperwork, then I'll be out to lend a hand. How does that sound?"

"I can handle that."

"Specials are on the board behind the register. Menus are on the tables already."

"Got it, boss lady." Ali gave a silly salute and headed out to the shop. She memorized the day's specials, donned the apron Valerie gave her, and had a quick lesson on the register. Lunch customers were just starting to filter in.

"Hi there. I'm Ali. What can I get for you?" she asked a small group of women that had seated themselves in the booth by the door.

"Ali?" one of the women asked.

"That's me."

"Ali, it's Tilly Miller. We went to high school together."

Ali wasn't surprised she hadn't recognized her. Her blond hair was now bright red, and it looked as though she had gotten a nose job. Either that or she had grown into her oversized beak. Ali doubted that was the case.

"Tilly. Nice to see you."

"I heard you left town without a word to anyone. Your parents up and left right after that. I always wondered if you were all running from the law or something."

Ali laughed politely. She hadn't liked Tilly in high school, and that hadn't changed. "No, nothing like that."

"As I recall you and Madison had been quite close. It surprised the heck out of us when she came out as a lesbian. Maybe you were trying to get as far away from that as you could. I wouldn't have blamed you."

This was Madison's business, Ali reminded herself. Be nice. "Not at all." She tossed around the idea of telling dear old Tilly that she was gay as well. But figured if she did that Tilly would more than likely put two and two together and come to the conclusion that she and Madison had been together. She didn't know if Madison would be okay with that or not. She bit her tongue. "What can I get for you ladies?"

"So why did you leave?" Tilly continued.

"I went to college, Syracuse University."

"Oh, no wonder you didn't come back. I would have left this crappy little town too if I hadn't married Ross Dell. Remember Ross, the football quarterback? All the girls had a crush on him. I'm sure you did too. He wanted to stay. He owns the biggest real estate business in the whole town."

Ali had the urge to defend Clyde. When she left, she'd blamed the town for her broken heart as much as she had blamed Madison. Since she'd been back, her small hometown had wormed its way back into her heart. "That's nice. Can I start you with something to drink?"

"So, you're back and you work here now, huh? Nice. I always thought you were going somewhere. Bet you never expected to end up back where you started."

That was all Ali could take. "I'll give you a few minutes to decide what you want. Just let me know when you're ready." She retreated before Tilly could say anything else. Madison came out of her office just as Ali reached the counter.

"You look like you're ready to blow a gasket," Madison said. "What's…" She glanced in the direction of Tilly and her friends. "Oh, let me guess. You waited on Tilly."

"How did you know that?"

"I swear she comes in here just to subtly insult me. Sometimes not so subtly. I'm sure she told you she married Ross and he owns the biggest real estate business in town."

"Yeah."

"It's the only real estate business in town. He inherited it from his father. Almost ran it into the ground at one point. She's a piece of work."

"Why do you take it?"

"Her money is just as good as anyone else's. Besides, it's bad for business when you start punching the customers in the face."

Ali laughed. Her mood lightened immediately. Madison still seemed to have that effect on her. "So, I'm not allowed to hit her?"

"I wish I could say yes. She's a homophobic snob. I'm sure she called you some gay slur."

"I didn't tell her I'm gay. I didn't know how you would feel if she linked us together."

"Ali, I decided to be true to who I am a long time ago. I don't care who knows or what their ignorant opinion is. You do you. Tell her or don't. That's up to you. But it doesn't bother me for people to know we used to be together. I was proud of what we were to each other."

Madison's attitude surprised Ali and warmed her soul.

"Looks like you are being summoned." Madison lifted her chin in Tilly's direction.

Ali glanced at Tilly's table. Tilly was waving the menu in the air, trying to get her attention.

"Want me to go wait on them?"

"Hell no. I've got this." She pulled the order pad from her apron pocket and headed back over to Tilly's table.

Madison had no doubt Ali could handle herself. She watched as Ali made her way over to Tilly's table, calmly took their order, and returned to the counter.

"How'd it go?" Madison asked.

"She ordered a tuna melt on rye. I told her that anything with tuna was a favorite among lesbians and did dear old Ross know she leans that way."

"You did not." Madison laughed. The exchange with Ali had a nostalgic feel to it. It felt like home.

"I did not." Ali joined in the laugher. "But it would have been fun if I did."

"I can't tell you how many times I wanted to tell her to go fuck herself. Maybe one of these days I will."

"That probably wouldn't be too good for business."

"Who knows? It might improve business if I stop serving homophobic bigots." But today was not the day for that. "You know what to do with the order now?"

"Wad it up and throw it out?"

"Close."

"I put it on this little turny thingy here. And spin it." Ali clipped the order where Valerie had shown her and turned it so the cook in the back preparing the food would get it.

"I'm glad you learned the technical terms. When the order is ready, Danny, the cook, will put the food on the shelf near the turny thingy thing and ring the little belly bell."

"Yep. Got it. Valerie done did teach me good."

In that moment of levity, Madison allowed herself to acknowledge just how much she had missed Ali. After months of Ali being gone, Madison had convinced herself that Ali meant nothing to her, and she was fine without her. It was the lie she told herself in order to survive the hurt. There was no need for that lie now. Ali was back and standing in front of her. At moments it seemed surreal. "Excellent. I'm done with the paperwork. You can take a break if you want."

"I only took one order. I don't think I need to rest quite yet."

"Yeah, but it was Tilly's order. That would tire anyone out."

The bell on the door jingled and a large group came through the door. Without asking, they pushed two tables together and proceeded to sit down. Madison recognized them as regulars. "I've got this," Ali said. "You are the one who should be taking it easy." She didn't wait for Madison to answer before waltzing over to the crowd.

The rest of the day went pretty much the same. Ali insisted that Madison take it easy and was quick to help wherever needed. They drove back to Madison's at the end of the workday, and Ali insisted that Madison sit while she made them dinner. When Madison insisted on helping, Ali relented enough to let her set the table.

"You seem to be doing a lot better," Ali said once they were seated.

"Thanks to you, I am."

Ali laughed, but it had an edge of nervousness to it. "I'm sure you would have healed without me. Anyway," she continued. "I'm sure you would like to get your house back to yourself. I'm thinking I should be heading home soon."

Madison's heart dropped to her stomach. She didn't want Ali to leave yet, but didn't blame her for wanting to get back to her life. "How soon?"

"Tomorrow."

Damn. That was very soon. Too soon. "I'll miss you." It was the truth.

"I'll miss you too. I would like to keep in touch if that's okay with you."

Of course, it was okay. Madison would have been disappointed if they didn't. "Absolutely."

They finished their meal in relative silence. The cloud that had suddenly arrived and floated over Madison's head drifted downward until it was settled in her heart, surrounding it in gray.

They worked together to load the dishwasher and Ali scrubbed the pans she had used to cook. "Want to watch a movie?" Madison asked her when they were done.

"Sure."

Madison settled on the couch and patted the spot next to her. She felt the need to have Ali close by. This would be their last night together and Madison was reluctant to let her go.

Ali sat down, leaving only a small space between them. Madison handed her the remote and turned off the lamp next to her. "You choose the movie."

Ali scrolled through the new releases on Netflix and settled on a movie with Nicole Kidman. "How's this?" she asked.

"Perfect." Madison reached over without much thought and intertwined her fingers with Ali's. Yes, she was really going to miss her. If Ali minded the gesture, she didn't show it. It wasn't long before Ali laid her head on Madison's shoulder. It appeared that Madison wasn't the only one feeling the need to be close. She found herself having a hard time concentrating on the movie. The warmth of Ali's hand in hers and the familiar feeling of Ali's head on her shoulder brought her back to younger days. Better days.

She wasn't sure if she should just enjoy the heat rising in her or extract herself from the situation. She still hadn't decided when Ali turned her head to say something and Madison squashed her words with her lips. Ali responded, pressing a tongue between Madison's lips until they parted, as if on their own, letting Ali have full access to her mouth. The heat rose faster than Madison could control it.

She slipped her hand under Ali's shirt and found what she was seeking. Ali's nipple hardened under her touch. A surge of moisture soaked her underwear and Madison needed them off. More than that, she needed Ali's off. She needed all of Ali's clothes off and wasted no time helping her out of them, breaking their kiss only long enough to pull Ali's shirt over her head. Madison's clothes soon followed and joined Ali's clothes on the floor. They made love with an urgency so intense it was as if their very existence depended on it. They lay in each other's arms, panting and spent, on the couch, Ali on top, her leg pressed between Madison's throbbing thighs.

Ali slowly extracted herself and slid down to the floor with her back propped up against the couch. Madison stroked her hair. She closed her eyes against the feelings that were stirring all over again.

"You okay?" Madison asked her.

More than okay. "Yes."

"I didn't plan that," Madison started to explain.

Ali didn't want an explanation. She wanted what they had just done to speak for itself.

"I'm going to miss you. I guess I got a little carried away with showing you that," Madison continued.

That was not what Ali wanted to hear. This wasn't the start of something like she wanted. It was the end. It was good-bye. At least Madison said she would miss her. That was something to cling to. Wasn't it?

Madison sat up, swinging her legs to the side to avoid hitting Ali. "I'm going to head up to bed." She swooped up her clothes and detangled them from Ali's. "See you in the morning." She went up the stairs without looking back, leaving Ali sitting on the floor, naked, stewing in her own thoughts.

What the hell just happened? Not that Ali didn't want it to happen. She did. She might have even started it. She wasn't sure. It was all a blur. What she didn't understand was why Madison ran away so quickly. Obviously, she regretted it. Ali refused to think of it as a mistake no matter how Madison felt. She'd wanted Madison as soon as she'd learned the truth about Howard. She would take this encounter and tuck it away in her heart, safe from the world and the dust.

She gathered her clothes, slipped them back on, and stayed downstairs until she was sure she had given Madison enough time to fall asleep. She crept up the stairs slowly, careful to avoid the one that squeaked. She tiptoed past Madison's closed door, changed into her pajamas, and slipped into bed. So many thoughts swirled through her head that she had trouble latching on to any for more than a second or two before the next thought landed on her doorstep.

One thing was clear, Madison was expecting her to leave tomorrow, like she said she was going to. Nothing that had just happened had changed that, as much as Ali wished it would. Wishes got her nowhere. They never did.

Madison heard Ali creep past her door and wondered why she hadn't come up sooner. She suspected it had everything to do with what they had just done and how Madison had run away. She hadn't known how else to handle it. Ali was leaving and Madison wasn't about to stand in her way.

She had a life to get back to. A life that seemed as far away as the other side of the world. A life that didn't include Madison. Madison had assumed, maybe wrongly, that Ali had wanted a new start. Another chance to be together. But she hadn't mentioned it again since their first meeting. She more than likely had changed her mind, especially after Madison had given no indication that it was even a possibility. And it probably wasn't.

As close to Ali as Madison felt, trying again would probably end in disaster. They had spent way too much time apart. They lived in different worlds now. Wanting to be with Ali, to touch her, to make love to her, was very different than wanting to be in a relationship. That's what Madison tried to convince herself. She knew she was a coward to run after being so intimate with Ali, but her emotions felt so raw, so exposed. She didn't want Ali seeing what was going on under the surface. She wasn't even sure what was going on under the surface. What she did know was that she cared for Ali and liked being with her. A lot. Beyond that she didn't have a clue.

Sleep was not her friend. With all the tossing and turning and thinking—so much thinking—she doubted she got more than two hours all night. She got up way before the usual time, determined to make breakfast for Ali instead of the other way around. She had the coffee made, the bacon cooked, and the scrambled eggs done. She expected Ali to be down before she had finished, but Ali wasn't down yet. She put the food in the oven, set it to warm and headed upstairs. The bathroom door was open, and the room was empty. She knocked on the guest bedroom door. No answer. She knocked again. "Ali?"

When Ali still didn't answer, she opened the door a crack and stuck her head in. The bed was made, and Ali was nowhere to be seen. "What the hell?" Madison said. She was about to go back downstairs when she spotted the folded piece of paper on the nightstand with her name on it.

"Oh shit." Madison sat on the bed and stared at the note as if it would bite her, afraid of what it held. She let out the breath she was holding and tentatively picked up the piece of paper and unfolded it.

Dear Madison,

Thank you. Thank you for forgiving me when I really didn't deserve it. Thank you for letting me stay with you, even when you didn't need me anymore. Thank you for letting me see who you are now. You have grown up to be a beautiful, remarkable, wonderful woman. You were all those things as a teenager, but even more so now.

Please don't be mad that I left without saying good-bye. It's a long drive back to Syracuse and I wanted to get an early start. Okay, that's not entirely true. I just couldn't face another good-bye with you. (Not that we had an actual "good-bye" when I left twenty years ago—my fault. I will forever be sorry about that.) Be good to yourself. You deserve it. And for God's sake, don't stress your back. I am so grateful for your existence in this crazy world.

Ali

Crap. I should have talked to her last night after what happened. Maybe she wouldn't have gone running. Or maybe I shouldn't have let it happen at all. Frustration built until it overflowed. Madison tucked the note in her pocket and headed back downstairs. She dumped the eggs and bacon into the trash. Her appetite had taken a hike, just like Ali had. The note said nothing about keeping in touch or Ali ever coming back. That wasn't what Madison had wanted. She wondered if there was a way to change that.

CHAPTER FIFTEEN

Charley threw his arms around Ali. "Why didn't you tell me you were coming home, honey child?" His pink sweatpants and matching T-shirt told Ali he had been planning a relaxing Sunday at home.

Ali wiggled out of his tight embrace. "I just decided yesterday."

"Baby, you must have left mighty early. It's barely noon. Come sit. Talk to me." Charley led her to the sofa and plopped down next to her. "Did something happen?"

Ali frowned.

"Oh. It did. Was it bad? Did you get into a fight? Did Madison Parker want you to leave?"

In his usual Charley way, he was asking questions without taking a breath so Ali could answer. She would just wait him out until he ran out of questions.

"Did you tell her you have strong feelings? Talk to me."

"Are you done?"

"For the moment," Charley answered. "Do you want a cup of coffee or…" He glanced at the clock on the wall. "A drink. It's not too early for a drink."

"No."

"No what?"

"No coffee and no drink. Yes, something happened. We had sex last night."

"Oh, sweetie, was it bad?"

"No. It was wonderful. At least for me. It brought up so many feelings. It reminded me of what we used to have. What I was missing with everyone after Madison."

Charley pulled his feet up under him on the couch. "Is that a bad thing?"

"Madison pretty much ignored what happened. She got up and went upstairs, barely speaking to me."

"Did you…" Charley paused.

Ali knew where the question was going. "No. She sort of started it. We were watching a movie on the couch and she held my hand."

"And that led to sex?"

"We started kissing. She was right there with me, a full participant. But something changed for her. I don't know what."

Charley took her hand. "Oh, baby. I'm sorry. That must have hurt." He looked down and raised their hands a couple of inches. "This, by the way," he said, gently shaking their clasped hands, "does not mean we're having sex."

Ali pulled her hand away. "Not funny."

"I'm sorry. I was just trying to make you smile."

Ali shook her head. "It's going to be a while before I feel like smiling again."

Charley hugged her. "That bad, huh?"

"That bad."

"What did Madison Parker say when you left this morning?" Charley got up and poured them both a glass of wine. Ali didn't object when he handed her a glass.

She took a gulp. "She was still asleep. I kind of—sort of— snuck out."

Charley sat down. "That doesn't sound like kind of sort of."

"I just couldn't face her. I shouldn't have let the sex happen. It changed something between us. I felt so close to her while it was happening and then so alone when she left me sitting on the floor naked."

A confused look flashed across Charley's face. "What?" Ali asked.

"I'm trying to decide if I should ask for more details or tell you that was TMI."

Ali swirled her glass and watched the wine leave a red trail in its wake. "No need to ask for more details because you aren't getting any. Suffice it to say that Madison must have regretted it as soon as it was over. Or she wouldn't have gone running like that."

"You ran too."

"I ran this morning after she wouldn't talk to me."

"Did you actually try to get her to talk to you? I mean did you attempt to talk to her about it?"

"I didn't get a chance. She left so quick."

Ali had replayed the exit scene over and over in her mind. There really had been no chance to talk. Not that she was sure what she would have said. Or maybe she did. She would have asked if there was a chance for them. A chance that they could work it out and be together again. And that was probably the exact reason Madison had run. It was a conversation she didn't want to have, because she didn't want Ali back.

"Do you think you want her back?" Jenny asked Madison.

"I didn't think so. No. I mean—I don't know. I really liked spending time with her. But I don't know."

"Sounds like you don't know."

"Don't know what?" Patty entered Jenny's kitchen carrying Grayson. He squirmed until she set him down and he went running to Madison.

"Hey, what about Gram Gram?" Jenny pouted.

"Gram Gram," Grayson squealed, but stayed in Madison's arms.

"Some of us got it," Madison said. "Some of us wish we had it."

"What don't you know?" Patty repeated.

Jenny handed her a stack of plates. "Set the table. I'm not sure Aunt Maddy wants to talk about it."

Patty stamped her foot. "Stop treating me like a five-year-old. Ooh, candy," she said, heading to the candy dish on the counter.

"Funny," Jenny said to her daughter.

"Where's your friend, Aunt Madison?"

"She went back home," Madison answered her. "She left this morning." Just saying the words weighed heavy on her heart as the guilt seeped in around the edges.

"That's too bad. I really liked her. So did Grayson. Like you said, some people got it."

Ali seemed to have it all right. Madison just wasn't sure what it was she had. Maybe it was a piece of her heart. Maybe a piece of her soul. Whatever it was she took it back to Syracuse with her. She had been gone less than a day and Madison felt like she had a hole inside her. She didn't like the feeling at all. It was good to be sitting down to dinner surrounded by family, but Madison couldn't help but notice that everyone else was paired off.

Jenny and Patty both had their husbands next to them. Of course, there was Grayson, sitting in a high chair between his parents. As cute as he was, he wasn't exactly Madison's dinner date type. She thought of how nice it would be to have Ali sitting next to her. Not just to have a body there, but to actually have Ali there.

"Where'd you go?" Jenny asked her, shaking her out of her thoughts.

"Nowhere. I'm right here."

"Patty asked you a question."

Shit. She had been too caught up in her thoughts and hadn't been paying attention. "The answer is yes, of course."

"Good to know," Patty said. "I asked if I got Grayson a puppy would you be willing to housebreak it for us."

Madison laughed. "Okay I wasn't listening. I wish to amend my answer to hell no."

Everyone laughed. Madison tried to push thoughts of Ali to the back of her mind, but she ended up hanging out in a thought bubble that hung just over her head, reminding her that Ali had gone home and that she missed her already. Madison gave a very sleepy Grayson a kiss on the top of his head. "Good night, little man." She hugged Patty and her husband good-bye. Jenny's husband, Jimmy, excused himself and went up to the office to do some work. Madison hung out in the kitchen with Jenny and helped put away the rest of the leftovers.

"Tell me for real how you're doing?" Jenny asked her as she covered a bowl of potatoes with plastic wrap.

"I'm okay. Why are you asking?"

"Because you're kind of—I don't know—in a fog."

Madison couldn't argue with that. She felt like she had drifted in and out of conversations all evening. "I'm just trying to sort out my feelings."

"About Ali?"

"Yeah."

"Did you come to any conclusions?"

"I don't know. It probably doesn't make a difference anyway." She grabbed an olive from the bowl before Jenny emptied it back into the jar.

"Why?"

"Because of the way Ali left. It was like she couldn't get away from me fast enough."

"What did you do?"

"And just why do you jump to the conclusion that I did something to her? I wasn't the only one naked on that couch you know."

Jenny stopped halfway to the fridge with the olives. "What? You kind of left out the part where you got naked and what happened after that."

Madison felt the heat creep up her neck. She knew she was turning a deep shade of red. She hadn't intended to tell Jenny what had happened between them. She knew Jenny well enough to know that now that the door was open, there was no way she was going to drop it without getting details.

Madison gave her a brief rundown, without giving too many details.

"You went upstairs without saying anything, like it didn't happen?" Jenny asked.

"I asked if she was okay and started to explain that I hadn't planned on having sex with her."

"That's it? You're intimate with the woman and that's what you say to her?"

"But—"

"Madison there is no but here. You were wrong. You are the one who ran. No wonder Ali left like she did. You don't have sex with someone who obviously cares about you as much as Ali does and then go to bed—alone—without acknowledging it. I can't believe you just left her there like that."

"That makes me an asshole doesn't it. I didn't know what else to do."

Jenny sat down and gave Madison her full attention. "Tell me what you were feeling."

"Mostly confused."

"About?"

"My feelings. Ali's feelings."

"Don't you think the thing to do would have been to ask her?"

"In hindsight, yes. At the time, I don't know. I felt so exposed, so vulnerable. I didn't want her to see that."

"For God's sake, Madison, you had just had sex with the woman. Of course, you would feel exposed and vulnerable. I'm sure she felt like that too."

"And I just left her there." How stupid and insensitive of her. She was starting to see Jenny's point. Madison had to find a way to make it right with Ali, if that was even possible.

Chapter Sixteen

It had been several days since Ali went home. Madison hadn't heard from her, and she wasn't surprised. She had spent a lot of that time reaming herself out for the way she had acted their last night together. She briefly considered driving to Syracuse and showing up at Ali's door. The fact that she didn't have her address would be a problem. She still hadn't sorted through all her feelings. The only thing she knew for sure was that she cared about Ali. Really cared. Maybe more than cared. That's the part she didn't have figured out. How much of her current feelings were real and how much were left over from twenty years ago? And did it even matter? If she was feeling it now it was real now. Wasn't it?

She felt like she was in a haze. It took all her energy when she was working to concentrate on the job at hand and the customers. As soon as she got home, she'd let her mind return to Ali and all the feelings that surrounded her and their time together. After days of thinking and many sleepless nights, she concluded that her feelings were real. They were now and they were then. It all blended together into a great big ball of raw nerve endings that yearned for Ali. Did Ali feel the same?

Madison didn't know, especially after the way Madison acted. She may have once, but that could have changed. She was back in her own life now. A life without Madison and the hurt that she had caused. A life she had been content in. Madison could have speculated forever. There was only one way to find out for sure. She pulled her phone from her pocket and placed it on the desk in front of her. She stared at it until she had formulated an opening dialogue in her mind and a list of points she wanted to make.

She jotted some notes down. Valerie and Lea could handle the shop for a little while. There was nothing stopping her from making the call—except fear. She set the timer on her phone for two minutes. That was how long she gave herself to get over it.

The phone rang long enough to go to Ali's voice mail. "This is Ali. Sorry I missed your call. If this is my editor, yes, I'm working on my rewrites. Everyone else, please leave a message. Don't expect a call back too soon, though. I'm working on my rewrites." Madison hung up the phone without leaving a message. She had practiced what to say when Ali answered. She didn't prepare a message.

"Oh, shit. I'm an idiot. How hard is it to say please call me?" Not hard. And yes, you are an idiot. Shut up, I don't need your opinion. No wonder Ali ran. Who wants to spend time with a crazy person who talks to herself? Sure, you can talk to yourself, but not to Ali. Hey! I'm trying here.

She hit Ali's number again in her contacts. This time she was prepared to leave a message. She was thrown off kilter when Ali answered the phone. "Hi, Ali, this is…" she started. "Ali?"

"Yes. Madison?"

"Yes. It's me. You threw me when you answered the phone." This is going well. Get your damn act together.

"You called me. Who did you expect to answer the phone?"

"You. Never mind. I meant to call you and it was you that answered the phone. So that's good." Not much better.

"Are you all right?"

Madison fiddled with the pens on her desk and knocked the notes she had written on the floor. "Yes. I'm fine. Well. No. Not really. I mean I'm sorry."

"What?"

"I'm sorry about what happened the night before you left."

"You are?" Madison could hear the disappointment in Ali's voice.

"No, no, not that part. I don't regret that we had sex." Made love? Maybe she should have said made love. Sex sounded so impersonal—and it was anything but impersonal. "I regret that I went upstairs and left you downstairs alone. I should have talked to you. I should have taken your hand and led you up to my room. What I did was wrong and I'm sorry."

No answer.

"Ali?"

No answer.

"Ali, can you say something?"

Ali wasn't sure what to think. She understood the apology part, but was Madison saying more than that? "Okay."

"Um, okay," Madison repeated. "How are you doing?"

"Fine." Her brain was still firing too rapidly to process correctly. Why exactly was Madison calling?

"Ali, I want you to come back."

If Ali felt off balance before, that statement sent her over the cliff. "What?"

"I want you to come back. I think there's some things we need to talk about. I don't want to do it over the phone. I can come there if that's easier for you."

"Can I get back to you on this?" Was she crazy? Madison just invited her back and she didn't jump at it. It was all she had wanted and now she hesitated. She was more confused than ever, not only by Madison, but also by her own answers.

"Of course. I'm sure you have a lot to catch up on now that you're home. I'll let you go, but please think about it."

"I will." Charley. She needed to talk to Charley to process this. "Thanks for calling."

"A…yeah…okay. Well. Good-bye, Ali." There was a pause. "Ali, I acted like an ass and I'm sorry."

"I'll call you later. Bye."

Ali hung up, not sure if Madison would have continued or not. What the hell was that? Ali felt like a yo-yo—as low as you can go when she left Clyde and Madison—starting the slow ascent back up in the last couple of days—and now spinning on the end of the string.

Ali closed her laptop. Her rewrites would have to wait. She needed to talk to Charley.

"I think if Madison Parker wants to see you, she should come here," Charley said after Ali explained what had happened. He added cream to his coffee from the little dish on the table. The coffee shop was nearly empty.

Ali was thankful for that. "Hmm."

"Do you want to see her?"

Ali took a sip of her coffee, giving her an extra couple of seconds to think. "I don't know." Obviously, a couple of seconds wasn't enough. "I mean I do. But what she did cut deep. I don't want to have to look into her eyes if she's going to tell me that what we did was a mistake and she doesn't want me in her life."

"Do you really think she would need to do that face-to-face? Wouldn't she just do that over the phone?"

"She might think she owes it to me to tell me in person. I don't know. This is so confusing."

"Honey child, what do you want to do? The hell with what Madison Parker wants. If you could write the script how would you want this to play out?"

The answer to that was easy. She wanted Madison back. They had lost too many years. She wished she could go back in time and have a do-over. That wasn't possible. Was it possible to start now and move forward together? Would Madison want that?

"Ali?"

"I want her back. Plain and simple. I don't know what she wants." She pushed her cup away from her. Her stomach had turned to acid, and even the smell of the coffee bothered her.

Charley ran a hand through the shock of bright pink hair on the top of his head. He had shaved the sides while Ali had been in Maryland. She wasn't sure if she liked it or not. "Honey, you need to tell her that. No matter what she wants to tell you, she needs to hear your feelings. If she doesn't want you after that, that's on her. But if you don't tell her, that's on you."

Charley had a point. She had kept her true feelings hidden from Madison. How could you blame someone for not responding to your feelings when you didn't share them? "You're right."

"I'm sorry. I didn't hear that. Can you say it again?"

Ali smiled at his good-natured teasing. Charley always did have a knack for making her feel better, if only in the moment. "I said you're right. I'll call her tonight and ask her to come here. That way we are on my turf and it won't be me running off with my tail between my legs if it goes south."

"Good plan, sweetie. You got this. Whatever happens, you can hold your head high and know that you were honest and did your best."

Ali nodded. She just hoped her best was good enough.

❖

Madison jumped at the sound of her ringing phone. Her conversation with Ali couldn't have gone worse. She had stumbled all over herself and couldn't get the words out right. So much for being prepared. Ali must have thought she'd lost her mind. A quick glance at the caller ID told her it was Ali calling back. She could almost feel her blood pressure rise. One deep breath in. One deep breath out. Repeat and answer the phone. "Hello."

"Hi, Madison." Pause. "You said you wanted to talk face-to-face and would be willing to come here. If you can take the time off from O's, I think that would be best." She sounded so formal. It was off-putting.

"Of course. I have Wednesday off. Does that work for you?" Please say yes.

"Yes. I'll text you the address. Do you know what time you would be arriving?"

"If I leave early, I could be there around noon."

"Okay."

"Ali, I…" Madison was at a loss for words. She didn't want to say too much now. She needed to see Ali face-to-face. "I'll see you Wednesday."

"Wednesday."

They said their good-byes and Ali hung up before Madison did. Maybe this was a mistake. Clearly, Ali didn't feel the same way she did. And Madison couldn't blame her. She might have blown any chance they might have had before they even started. Ugh. She needed to stop these crazy revolving thoughts. They were getting her nowhere. She would tell Ali how she felt. She would need to clarify the wording in her own mind and be better prepared. And of course, she needed to tell her how sorry she was for abandoning her. Yes. She would start there and see how Ali felt. If Ali didn't feel the same—game over. If she did, they could figure out how to take the next steps together. Madison sure hoped there would be next steps to take.

❖

Madison turned the radio down as she turned onto Ali's street, as if she needed quiet to find the right apartment building. It must have helped because she spotted it right away. Of course, it was made easier by the fact that it appeared to be the only apartment building on the street. The small parking lot boasted four spots marked for individual apartments and several spots designated for visitors. Ali's was the only car in the lot.

The building looked like it was once a large mansion that had been converted to apartments. The wooden exterior appeared well cared for. Gardens with daffodils finishing up their season lined the sidewalk leading to the front door. Madison pushed her nerves aside and rang the bell with Ali's name on it. Within seconds, she heard a buzz and was able to push the door open and make her way to Ali's apartment on the second floor. The door opened before she had the chance to knock. Just seeing Ali again took her breath away. She had on a light blue button-up shirt, snug jeans, and just enough makeup to make Madison want to kiss her. Or maybe Madison just wanted to kiss her—makeup or not. But she didn't. They needed to talk, not end up naked again—at least not yet.

"Hi," Ali said tentatively.

"Hi. Thanks for letting me come."

"Sure." Ali stepped back to let Madison in. The apartment felt warm and inviting. The living room furniture looked simple yet comfortable. The few pictures on the wall looked like real paintings, not prints. An award for one of Ali's books sat unassuming on top of the bookcase. It looked like Ali had done well for herself, just like she had said.

"Sit down. Make yourself comfortable. Would you like something to drink?"

The couch was as comfortable as it looked. Madison chose it over the chair in the hope that Ali would sit closer, making it easier to talk. "Sure. Whatever you have is fine. Wine would be great if you don't think it's too early."

Ali smiled. "Never too early for wine."

That was a good sign. Even if she hated Madison, she still liked wine. Madison laughed at that thought. Her nerves were getting to her. She planned to be cool, state her case, apologize, of course, and listen to Ali's thoughts. Her coolness seemed to be going out the window.

Ali disappeared into the kitchen and emerged with two glasses of red wine. She handed one to Madison and sat down on the couch, leaving a couple of feet between them. Madison sipped her wine, stood up, and went to the bookcase by the wall. She pointed to the award. "I'm impressed," she said. She nonchalantly made her way back to the couch and sat down, eliminating some of the space between them. Her coolness had returned. "First," she started.

"No."

"No?"

Ali took a large sip of her wine, making Madison wait for her response. "No. I want to go first."

"But I—"

"Please, Madison. Let me say this before I lose my nerve."

Madison realized that Ali was just as nervous as she was. "Okay." She reached for Ali's hand but stopped short of taking it. She rubbed her hand on her pants instead, hoping Ali didn't notice.

Ali was glad Madison didn't continue her attempt to take her hand. The physical connection might have been too much in the moment. She needed to tell Madison how she felt, without any distractions. "What you did after we had…" she trailed off. This would be harder than she thought. "...sex," she continued. "It hurt. A lot. I felt used."

"That's what—"

Ali held up her hand. She needed to get this out. "That's how I felt afterward. I want to tell you how I felt before that."

"Okay."

"I felt like I was falling back in love with you." Ali swallowed. "Being around you, talking, joking, being so close to you, it was—it was heaven. It felt so good. We made love. You can call it sex if you want, but it was more than just a physical act to me." She looked away to try to gain her composure. She was close to tears. The last thing she wanted to do was cry in front of Madison. Again. "I thought maybe we had a chance in that moment. Then you get up and leave. Just like that. Any hopes of a future left when you left that room." She swiped at a tear that disobeyed her orders and trailed down her cheek.

"And now?" Madison asked.

"Before I answer that, I have a question for you."

Madison nodded.

"Did being intimate with me mean anything to you?"

"Of course, it did. Ali, I was confused. I was having feelings I didn't want to have."

"Good to know you didn't want to have feelings for me." Another errant tear. Damn it.

"That's not what I mean. You came back into my life without warning. I wasn't prepared for that. I told myself a long time ago that I didn't need you. That you meant nothing to me. Ali, I thought you left me because what we had didn't mean anything to you. That took a long time to get over. I sure as hell wasn't ready to jump back in feet first."

"I get that—"

"My turn now," Madison said more harshly than she intended. "I'm sorry," she said, consciously trying to soften her voice. "I just want you to understand. All of a sudden, you were there and all I wanted was for you to leave."

The look on Ali's face told her to get to the part where she cared, because so far all she was doing was hurting Ali more.

"But that changed. You helped me when you didn't have to. But things didn't change because I needed to rely on you. They changed because I was around you again and I was reminded of how wonderful you are."

With that, Ali's face softened.

"The bottom line here is they changed, Ali. My feelings for you changed."

"Why did you leave me there, sitting on the living room floor alone."

This time Madison did take Ali's hands in hers. "I don't know."

Ali pulled her hands away. "Wrong answer." She stood and turned her back to Madison.

Madison rushed to explain. "I was confused. All the feelings that were rushing through me were too much. They weren't bad feelings. They were good, but they were strong."

Ali turned around and faced Madison. "And what about my feelings?"

"You said you were leaving. I didn't think you had strong feelings for me. Not anymore."

"We had just made love. Do you think I do that with just anyone?"

"Of course not. I…" It was so hard to explain, but she had to make Ali understand. "I…"

"You what?" Ali was losing patience.

"Ali, can you sit down? Please. I'm trying to tell you how I felt. I'm sorry I'm not doing it good enough. Please."

Ali sat, leaving space between them.

"I got scared. You were going home to your own life and I was going back to mine. Having feelings for you didn't fit neatly into that scenario. I was scared and confused. Can you understand that?"

Ali let the silence between them grow until it was big enough to swallow Madison whole. There were no more words she could think to say that would explain it any better.

"Done?" Ali asked at last.

"I'm not confused or scared anymore." It had taken days and tons of thinking to figure out what she wanted. "I want to try again with you. How do you feel about that?"

Ali bit the inside of her cheek. Madison recognized the habit as something Ali did when they were young, and Ali was deep in thought. Madison sat quietly, patiently waiting while Ali thought about Madison's confession. She didn't have to wait long.

"How can I trust you now?"

"The same way I came to trust you again after you left. You didn't answer my question. How do you feel about me now? About the possibility of us?"

Ali shook her head, and Madison's heart sank. "It's hard."

"Of course, it's hard. Life is hard. But maybe it doesn't have to be quite as hard together." Madison laughed. "I never thought it would be me trying to convince you." So much had changed in the last few weeks. Changes Madison never expected. Changes she hadn't handled well so far. Now was the time to change that. "What else can I say to make you believe me?"

"I believe you. That's not the problem. You ran when things got confusing and scary for you. That scares me now."

"Not to throw it in your face, but you ran first."

"I was eighteen years old. I was a stupid kid." She grabbed her glass of wine and held it up as if she was cheering, before gulping some down.

"And I'm a stupid thirty-eight-year-old. That's the only excuse I've got." She wasn't going to beg. "Please, Ali. Please." Or maybe she was.

"My feelings didn't change."

That's what Madison wanted—needed—to know. They could work together to rebuild a relationship if they both had feelings for each other. "So, there's a chance." It was more of a statement than a question.

Ali didn't answer. Madison wished she could read her mind, like she could sometimes do when they were younger. "Is there a chance?"

Cheek bite again. "We need to take it slow."

Yes. There was a chance. "I can do slow. I can do it any way you need to do it." She had just handed all her power to Ali, and she was totally okay with that.

Ali finished her wine in three more gulps.

"Where do we go from here?" Madison asked.

"Where do you want to go?"

To your bedroom. "How about I take you out to dinner? A date. A real date."

"We can do that. But I have to warn you, I'm going to order the most expensive thing on the menu."

Madison laughed. "You order anything you want. I am an extremely semi-successful entrepreneur with my own business." She paused. "I'll take out a loan."

Now it was Ali's turn to laugh. The sound went right to Madison's heart and lit it up from within. She was so glad they were able to lighten the mood. Her decision to come to Syracuse and tell Ali how she felt was the right one.

"I am an extremely successful *New York Times* best-selling author. I can float you a loan if you need it."

"You are not," Madison said, sure Ali was teasing her.

The cutest shade of red colored Ali's cheeks. "Actually, I am."

"What? You are?"

"I am."

"Why didn't you tell me that before?"

"It seemed like bragging. But now that I know you may need extra money to buy me a fancy meal, I figured it was time to come clean."

"Thank you," Madison said. She took a sip of her wine. The warmth it stirred in her belly was matched by the warmth Ali stirred in her heart.

CHAPTER SEVENTEEN

Madison left saying she would be back at six thirty to pick Ali up for dinner. Ali had trouble concentrating on her rewrites. She closed her laptop, clasped her hands behind her head, and leaned back in her office chair. She closed her eyes and lazily turned her chair in circles.

The conversation with Madison played through her mind. Had she said everything she needed to say? Should she have said anything different? Did she let Madison off the hook too easy? No. She didn't think she did. Madison seemed truly sorry. Ali had prepared herself for a final good-bye from Madison. She was relieved that didn't happen and surprised that Madison wanted to try again. Surprised and extremely happy. She smiled to herself and took another spin around in her chair.

She was ready way before Madison arrived. Happy to have her whole wardrobe to choose from, she decided on black dress pants, tucked into knee-high boots, a light blue shirt with dark blue trim that hung loose enough to be forgiving, but had a plunging neckline. She had trouble finding the right bra that would show off her cleavage, give her enough support, and yet be out of sight. She finally found it tucked in the back of her underwear drawer. Her necklace and earrings matched the blue in her shirt, and she added the slightest touch of blue eyeshadow to her carefully made-up face. She nodded at her reflection in the mirror. "You got this."

She gave Charley a quick phone call to update him on the latest developments.

"I am so happy for you, baby girl. Just relax and have fun tonight. The weight of the world doesn't depend on this date. Think of it as a new beginning." Once again, Charley knew exactly what to say. "And don't do anything I wouldn't do."

"That pretty much means I can do anything, 'cause, there isn't much you wouldn't do."

"Got that right, sister. I expect a full report tomorrow."

"I know the drill. I better finish getting ready. Talk to you soon. Bye." She hung up and went in search of her shoulder wrap. It was hiding in the front closet, right where it should be. Madison arrived on time, a beautiful bouquet of flowers in hand. Ali suspected she might have sat in her car so that she walked in exactly at six thirty. It was something Ali would do.

"Wow," Madison said. "You look great. These are for you." She handed Ali the flowers. There were three red roses in the mix. Ali's favorite.

"Thank you. You look pretty wonderful yourself." Madison was wearing a button-down shirt with several buttons undone, showing a generous amount of skin. Ali realized she was staring and brought her eyes up to Madison's. Those gorgeous brown eyes.

"Are you ready to go? We have reservations for seven."

Ali was surprised. "You made reservations?"

"I want to do this right. I found the nicest restaurant in town—I hope. Their lobster and steak, the most expensive thing on the menu, is five-star rated."

Ali wasn't sure if Madison was telling the truth or teasing her. She would have been happy with Burger King, although she was a little overdressed for that.

"Let me just find a vase for these." Ali had no idea if she even owned a vase. She was more the flower giver than the flower receiver in her previous relationships. She finally found a heavy beer stein in her cupboard that would do. She knew enough to clip the bottoms of the stems before submerging them in the water.

"Wait," Madison said as Ali was about to open the door.

Ali turned to her. "What?"

Madison put her hands on each side of Ali's shoulders and gently pulled her in. She planted a light kiss on Ali's lips. "I would like to acknowledge that I just kissed you. And I liked it."

Ali laughed, pulled Madison closer by her collar, and kissed her hard enough to leave her lips a deeper shade of red and looking a bit swollen.

"And I liked that even more," Madison said when Ali finally let her loose.

"I'm glad we can talk about it."

"I'm the only one doing the talking."

"I liked it too. A lot."

"I think this new start is going great so far." Madison smiled.

"It is. The first fifteen minutes have been good."

"Only good?"

"Great." She pulled Madison in for one more kiss. "Really great."

The restaurant valet opened the car door. Madison slipped out of the seat and handed him her keys. She hadn't been joking. This was one of the nicest places in Syracuse. Ali had never eaten here but had heard great things about it and knew it was expensive. A stone walkway, limestone, Ali guessed, led to a set of glass frosted doors, etched with the name of the establishment. She was impressed and they hadn't even walked in yet.

They were seated right away, bypassing several couples waiting for tables. The double-sided fireplace in the center of the restaurant gave off a warm, subtle scent of burning wood. "How did you manage this on such short notice?" Ali ran her hand over the woven white tablecloth.

"I managed. I sold my soul, but you're worth it." Madison smiled at her.

"I'm not sure I want a soulless girlfriend."

"Girlfriend? I like that."

"It's the soulless part that I'm worried about."

The waitress appeared to take their drink orders. Ali was determined not to drink too much. She needed to keep her wits about her. That also assured them a safe ride home if Madison happened to have one too many. "I lied," Madison said.

That got Ali's attention.

"I didn't really sell my soul."

Ali pretended to wipe her brow. "That's a relief. Was it your body? Did you sell your body? Because I have to tell you that is some body. You probably could have gotten several reservations and maybe even a few free meals with it."

"No. I am saving myself for you. Only you, no matter how many free meals I'm offered."

All this talk about Madison's body sent a surge of electricity through Ali that landed squarely in her center. Her mind went back to the last night she spent at Madison's house and Madison naked underneath her. She swallowed hard and couldn't help but smile.

"What's that grin for?" Madison asked.

"Just thinking about your body. It is a wonderland."

"That sounds like a song."

"It is a song. Want me to sing it to you?"

"I bring you out to a nice restaurant and you threaten me with that?"

Ali laughed. Their wine arrived in record time saving Madison from listening to her sing.

The waitress listed off the specials, recommending the seared salmon with lemon butter.

"Is there onion or garlic in that?" Ali asked. The last thing she wanted tonight was garlic breath.

"No, ma'am."

"I'll have that."

"I thought you wanted something fancy?" Madison said.

"I live a simple life. Salmon is fancy to me." Ali smiled and was rewarded with a smile in return. It lit up Madison's face, making her even more beautiful.

Madison ordered the same. "I'm so glad we're here," she said to Ali once they were alone again. "I meant everything I said today, Ali. I want to give this all I've got."

"I appreciate that. I'm willing to do the same." Ali wasn't sure how it was going to work, seeing as they lived three hundred and thirty-two miles apart—the exact distance from her door to Madison's door. But somehow, they would work it out. She was sure of it. She pushed away thoughts about obstacles and gave her full attention to Madison.

"Tell me about your books being on the New York Times Best Seller list."

"There's not much to tell. My third book made the list and three books after that did as well. It helps with sales."

"Why are you so modest? I would be screaming it from the rooftops."

Ali sipped her wine and considered her answer. "I haven't really thought about it before. I think I've just been floating through life, not really clinging to anything. That would include my books. I write them and send them into the world on their own to sink or swim. Luckily, they have done well."

"It must be more than luck. You must have skill. Do you still feel like you're floating?"

"You certainly ask some deep questions."

"I want to know you again, Ali. It's important to me. You're important to me." Ali smiled. She liked Madison's questions and wanted to give her honest answers. It helped her to be honest with herself as well, something she hadn't been doing for a long time. "I felt more grounded when I was back in Clyde than I have in a long time. It anchored me. If I'm really being honest, you anchored me."

"Was it hard leaving and coming back here?"

"The hard part was leaving you. Syracuse has been fine. Not a bad place to live. But it feels less like home since I've been back."

"What keeps you here?"

Ali hadn't done this much soul searching in a long time. She had been trying to figure out her feelings since she'd arrived back. Madison's questions helped her figure things out in a way her own questions hadn't been quite able to do. "Charley." Plain and simple. That was all she really valued here.

"Are you in love with him?" Was that a bit of jealousy in Madison's voice?

Ali's laugh came out like a snort. "Charley is not my type. The penis thing gets in the way. I'm as gay as they come." She paused. "He's been my best friend since college. I love him. But in love with him? No."

Their food arrived and the smell of fresh salmon and lemon filled the air around them. Ali took a bite. It tasted as good as it smelled. They fell into a comfortable silence as they enjoyed their food.

Madison broke the quiet after several bites. "The letter you sent me—and the other women you've had relationships with…"

Ali put her fork down. "Yes."

"You had said you only had it partially figured out. Did you ever figure out the rest—why your relationships weren't successful? Did you get the answers you were after?"

"It took a while and a trip back to Maryland, but yes. I was the reason."

"What do you mean?"

"I realized that I didn't consider myself important in the relationships. I just went along for the ride, always letting the other person drive. They didn't work because I wasn't really into them."

"That's sad."

"The thing I've figured out is I am important. My wants, my needs, they matter. I am never going to settle again. I've done that too many times. I want a true partnership."

"Of course, you're important. Why did you think you weren't?"

"How is everything?" the waitress was back, interrupting their conversation. It gave Ali a little extra time to figure out the best way to answer Madison's question.

"Excellent," Madison answered.

"Anything else I can get for you?"

"I think we're all set. Ali?"

Ali shook her head.

Madison repeated her question once the waitress left. "When I thought you chose someone else over me, it cut me. I felt like a piece of me was gone. Like I didn't deserve to be who I am."

Madison reached across the table and took Ali's hand. The warmth of it spread through Ali. "I'm so sorry. I had no idea."

"How could you? I did it to myself. I built a shield around myself and chose people..." Ali stopped and considered her words. "No. That's not right. I didn't choose. I let people choose me. But I had no real interest in letting them in. It was safer that way."

"And now—with me?"

"Madison, you've always been in my heart. I don't have to work on letting you in, because you never left."

It occurred to Ali that the only other person she'd had deep conversations with, in many years, was Charley. She'd never talked to any of her girlfriends like this, so raw, so exposed and at the same time, so safe.

"Ali, I feel the same. You've always been with me. I just built a wall around those feelings to protect myself from the pain. I took my time taking that wall down, brick by brick. The more time we spent together, the more bricks came down."

"Are there any bricks left?"

Madison seemed to roll the question around in her mind. "I would like to say no, but the truth is, I think there are still a couple there. The mortar around them is gone, so the foundation is weak. It won't take much to knock them down."

"I appreciate your honesty. That was very creatively said, by the way. Maybe you should be a writer too."

Madison laughed. "I don't think so. I'll leave that to you. Someone has to make the donuts in this world."

"True. This would be a sad place without donuts."

The dinner and the company were stellar. They pulled into Ali's parking lot and Madison walked Ali to her door. "I had a wonderful time tonight," Madison said.

"Would you like to come in for a nightcap?"

"Absolutely."

Ali unlocked the door and Madison followed her in. "Where are you staying?" They hadn't discussed sleeping arrangements and Ali assumed she had a hotel room. She couldn't imagine that Madison had gotten herself ready for their date in a gas station restroom or her car.

"The Holiday Inn."

"Is your stuff already there or is it in your car?" Should she ask Madison to stay the night—in the guest room?

"There."

Madison obviously hadn't planned on them spending the night together either. It left Ali feeling a little conflicted. On one hand she was glad Madison hadn't assumed anything. And on the other she was a little disappointed that Madison hadn't assumed anything.

"Wine?" Ali asked.

"Water would be fine."

"Sit." Ali fetched them both a glass of water. She set them down on the coffee table and sat next to Madison on the couch.

"I would like to kiss you," Madison said. "If that's okay with you."

Ali tapped her chin. "Hmm. Yes. I guess that would be okay."

Madison kissed her lightly on the cheek.

"Well, that was disappointing," Ali said.

"You've had better?"

"You've done better."

"Can I have a do-over?"

Ali handed Madison her glass of water. "Here. Drink this, while I think about it."

Madison had barely taken a sip when Ali snatched the glass out of her hand, spilling a few drops on the coffee table as she set it back down. "I thought about it and you can have a do-over." Without waiting for a response, she kissed Madison full on the mouth.

"Now that is a kiss," Madison said when Ali let her up for air. "I see what you mean. How's this?" She kissed Ali on the cheek again, longer and with more pressure.

"Nope. You still don't have it. You need to add some tongue action in."

Madison gave her another kiss on the cheek that ended with her flicking her tongue across Ali's skin.

Ali wiped her cheek and laughed. "I think you need more practice. You don't quite have it down yet."

Madison wrapped her arms around Ali, pulled her in close, and kissed her deeply. Ali's body responded like a drowning person would respond to a full breath of air. She was trembling by the time Madison finished.

"How was that?"

Ali had trouble speaking. "Fine," she managed to squeak out.

"More practice?"

"Practice is good."

Madison kissed her again, her tongue sweeping across Ali's lips until they parted, giving Madison full access. Ali's brain shut down as her body came alive. She pulled Madison closer and raked her fingers through her hair. The kiss continued until Ali moved her hands to Madison's breasts.

Madison pulled back. "I'm not going to be able to stop if you keep doing that."

"Who said I want you to stop?" Ali attempted to pull Madison back in.

"You said you wanted to take it slow. This is not taking it slow."

"I've changed my mind." She attempted to pull Madison back into the kiss again.

"Ali, I don't want to do anything to mess this up. As much as I want you—and I do want you—we should wait."

"Why?" The heat in Ali's body engulfed her. Her center was on fire.

"I'm sure there was a reason, but I can't think of it right now." Madison sat back, moving farther away from Ali. "I need space so I can remember it."

Ali filled the gap between them and lightly kissed Madison on the mouth. "Are you thinking?"

"That is not helping."

"So sorry." She kissed her again with a little more pressure. "We should get to know each other all over again. That was the reason. I remembered it."

"What do you want to know?" Ali planted small kisses along Madison's jawline and down her neck, the skin soft under her lips.

"If you had a goldfish, what would you name her? Can you even tell if it's a her?"

Ali's kisses trailed off and she sat up. "What are you doing?"

"I'm trying to figure out if this is a good idea."

"And questions about an imaginary goldfish helps how?"

"Ali, what happens tomorrow if we do this now?"

"Tomorrow we do it again. Do you not want this? Am I making assumptions here?" She wasn't sure she wanted to hear the answer. Madison took Ali's hand and placed it over her heart. "What does this tell you?" Madison's heart was pounding, and Ali thought it might jump out of her chest at any moment. "I want this. I want to make sure it's what you really want, and you won't regret it in the morning."

"As long as you are still here in the morning, I won't regret it." She searched Madison's eyes for the truth.

"I won't ever desert you like that again. I promise."

"Then I want this."

Madison needed no further prompting. She pushed Ali backward and climbed on top of her.

"Stop."

Madison pushed herself up. "What?"

"Bedroom."

Madison followed Ali to her room. It was as simple and as comfortable looking as the living room had been, except for numerous decorative pillows cluttering the bed. Ali took no time sweeping them to the floor and pulling back the covers.

Madison brought her focus back to the woman before her. She was done asking. Done hesitating. She unzipped Ali's pants and slipped her hand inside, between Ali's thighs. Ali was wet. Oh, so deliciously wet. She stroked Ali with her thumb and slipped a finger inside her. Ali's moan told her all she needed to know.

Ali's mouth was on her neck, licking and sucking as Madison pushed her fingers into her swollen flesh below. They stopped long enough to shed their clothes and Madison slid a single finger across Ali's folds and into her again and plunged her tongue into Ali's eager mouth. Without breaking contact, Madison walked Ali back toward the bed, wrapped her free arm around her back, and gently lowered her before crawling in on top of her. She replaced her hand with her leg and pressed it hard between Ali's thighs.

Ali kissed her with the same passion that Madison felt. Her kiss became more insistent as her tongue entered Madison's mouth. A moan came up from deep within Madison and was quickly swallowed by Ali. Their tongues fought for space in a dance around each other.

The wetness in Madison's center grew with each thrust of her leg.

Ali let out another gasp as Madison replaced her leg with her fingers again. Ali's juices were slick and warm, and Madison's finger slipped in and out easily. She increased her speed and pressure as she felt Ali's passion rise. Ali pulled her mouth away and let out a sound, deep from her throat as her muscles tightened around Madison's fingers and she came in a rush. Her pleasure became Madison's pleasure and Madison clamped her own legs together against the sensation. Ali tightened her arms around Madison for several long seconds. She found Madison's mouth again and kissed her.

"Whoa," Ali said when she seemed to find her voice again.

"Good?" Madison eased herself off Ali, and onto her side. She pulled Ali in close and buried her face in Ali's hair.

"That's an understatement. Give me a minute and I'll see if I can return the favor."

Madison pulled the blankets up around them. She was content where she was. "Take your time. I'm just enjoying having you in my arms." She felt warm and safe and loved. She hoped her arms made Ali feel the same. It wasn't long before Ali's breathing told her she had fallen asleep. Madison snuggled in and closed her eyes. She didn't know how long she had been out when she was awakened by Ali's hand stroking between her legs.

"Sorry," Ali whispered.

Madison cleared her throat to dislodge the sound of sleep. "For what?"

"For falling asleep on you."

"My fault. I must have worn you out." She let out a gasp as Ali pushed a finger into her.

"My turn to wear you out. I want you to have a good night too."

Ali pushed the blankets off Madison and replaced her fingers with her mouth. Her breath was warm on Madison's thigh, her tongue velvety soft against her. She pressed a finger inside Madison and then added a second. Madison lost all awareness of anything except the glorious feelings that Ali was stirring. She felt the pressure inside her center build as Ali stroked and licked her into ecstasy. She squeezed her eyes shut and bit down on her lip as an explosion of sensations ripped through her. Her breath caught in her throat as a second round started. Ali didn't let up until Madison came down from a third orgasm.

She gently extracted Ali's fingers, pulled Ali's face up to her and kissed her, tasting her own juices on Ali's lips. She was turned on all over again. They made love several times, dozing in between, and waking up only to start all over again. The sun was just starting to peek through the bedroom curtains when they finally fell into a deep sleep in each other's arms.

Ali woke first, content to watch Madison sleep. "Good morning, beautiful," she said when Madison finally opened her eyes.

"Hi there."

"I need a shower," Ali said.

"That's a sexy thought to wake up to."

"Would you like to join me?"

"Oh yeah."

Ali smiled. She never thought she would have Madison back in her arms like this.

"Ali?"

"Yes."

"I'm sorry for what I did the last time we were together. I'm sorry for the storm I caused in your heart."

"I know. The storm wasn't fun, but the rainbow sure is awesome."

Madison kissed her full on the mouth. It was an hour before either one of them stepped into the shower. And another hour before they stepped out of it.

Chapter Eighteen

"When do I get to meet Charley?" Madison asked. They had just finished the breakfast Madison had insisted on making them.

"You want to meet Charley?" Ali asked, surprised.

"Unless you don't want me to. Why don't you want me to? Is there something wrong with him? Are you embarrassed of him? Are you embarrassed of me? Are you afraid he'll like me more than you? That's it, isn't it? You'll be jealous."

"You're crazy, you know that?" She kissed Madison on the lips and stood to clear the table. "You can meet him anytime you want. I'm just surprised. That's all."

"He's important to you, so he's important to me."

Ali stacked the plates and set the silverware on top of the pile. "We can see if he's free for lunch. He should be working but gets a break at noon."

Madison stood, pulled her phone from her back pocket, and looked at the time. "Considering it's almost eleven and we just finished breakfast, I don't think I'll be hungry in an hour."

Ali kissed her again. "I will. I need extra energy for what I plan on doing to you later."

"It can't be much later. I'll have to get on the road by six. I have to be up early for work tomorrow."

Ali's heart sank. She had been so happy to have Madison here that she didn't think about when she had to leave. "Do you have to go?" Ali tried to keep her voice from sounding whiny.

Madison put her arms around Ali's waist and leaned her head on her shoulder. "I do. I don't want to." She looked up at her. "You can come with me."

There was nothing Ali would have liked more. She could work from anywhere, but was it wise to be going back to Clyde so soon? She was just starting to settle back in at her apartment. So many things ran through her mind, how good it would be to spend more time with Madison, how productive or unproductive she would be on her rewrites if she was in Clyde, how she would miss Charley leaving so soon after she got back. Staying put and doing the long-distance thing for a while might be a smarter thing to do.

"What do you think, Ali?"

"I think I would love to be with you."

"Good. It's settled then." Madison smiled that smile that made Ali's heart melt.

"But…"

"No, no, no. No but."

"But," Ali continued. "I should stay here and finish working on my book. I'm not sure I could do it knowing you were close by, serving donuts in that sexy way you do."

"You think my donut serving abilities are sexy?"

"I think everything you do is sexy. The way you smile, the way you dress, the way you make breakfast, and especially the way you serve donuts."

"Very astute of you to notice," Madison said.

"Oh, I noticed all right."

"When will I get to see you again?"

"How about I come down in a couple of weeks?"

"I would like that. A lot."

"Then it's a plan. I'll call Charley to see if he's free at noon, if you still want to meet him." Ali liked the idea of the most important people in her life meeting each other.

❖

"I love your makeup," Madison said to Charley, decked out in dark dress pants and a hot pink blouse with puffy sleeves. She wasn't sure what to expect when Ali told her about him. He didn't sound like anyone she'd ever met before, and she realized how sheltered her small-town life was sometimes. Something she should probably correct. Charley turned out to be warm and welcoming. Not that Madison was surprised. He had to be something special to be so important to Ali.

"Thank you, love. I get a nice discount working at Ive's."

"Charley demos their makeup for them in the mall," Ali explained.

They made their way to the farthest picnic table and sat down.

Charley set his tray of food down in front of him. "Are you sure you don't want something to eat? I got extra fries so that I could share." He pushed them to the middle of the table.

Madison waved them away. "No, thanks. We had a late breakfast. But you go ahead and enjoy your lunch." She took a sip of her soda. "I'm so glad you could meet us on your break today."

"Child, it's my pleasure. I wanted to meet the famous Madison Parker." He flashed her a big smile before diving into his burger.

"Famous or infamous?" Madison asked. She was sure Charley had heard an earful about her, not all of it good.

"Stop it," Ali said and kissed her on the cheek.

"If Ali's happy, I'm happy," Charley said. "I see the smile on her face. She's obviously happy."

"I'm going to do my best to keep it that way," Madison said.

"That's all I can ask." He dipped a fry in the little paper cup of ketchup. "Ali tells me you make the best chocolate cream donuts on the whole East Coast."

Madison laughed. "I doubt Ali's tasted all of the chocolate cream donuts on the whole East Coast."

"I didn't have to. I know quality when I taste it," Ali said.

"It's actually my dad's recipe. We haven't changed it in…" Madison had to think about it. "Hmm. Thirty years."

"I have to ask," Charley said. "Where did the name O's come from? Is it because donuts are shaped like o's?"

Madison relayed the story to him. "I love it. That makes more sense than having it named after the big O. That's what Ali thought it was."

Ali threw a wadded-up napkin at him. "You lie. I did not."

"Ow." Charley rubbed his arm where the napkin hit. "I'm delicate—like a flower. A delicate little daisy. You better hope that doesn't leave a mark."

Madison laughed. "I can see why Ali likes you so much."

"What's not to like?" Charley waved his hand in the air.

The time seemed to fly by. Charley emptied his tray into the trash and returned it to the burger stand. He gave Madison a tight hug. "Treat my baby girl right," he whispered in her ear.

"I promise," she whispered back.

"I like him," Madison said after they dropped him back off at work.

"Yeah. He's the best. He's always been there when I needed him."

"I'm glad you had him."

"What would you like to do today?" Ali asked. "We have a nice zoo, the Erie Canal Museum, Green Lakes is really nice. I know your time is limited. I'd like to show you some of Syracuse."

"Why do they call it Green Lakes?"

"Because it's green."

"Ha ha, lakes aren't green, unless it's got a ton of algae or it's polluted."

"No really. It looks green and it's not polluted. There are high levels of calcium carbonate which somehow makes the water look green." Ali laughed. "I really should know more than that, living here for twenty years. I do know it's beautiful. We could hike or rent a rowboat. There are some nice restaurants right near there, so we could take in an early dinner before you have to hit the road. What do you think?"

Madison hadn't been running since she hurt her back. Getting out in nature and going on a nice walk would do her good. Having Ali by her side would make it all the better. "A hike sounds great. Are you into hiking? I don't even know." There was a lot of things she didn't know about Ali. Yet.

"It's just like walking, right? I know how to walk."

Madison laughed. "Yeah. That works. Just make sure you are wearing something comfortable on your feet."

Ali held up her foot, showing off her sneaker. "I always do."

A quick stop at Ali's for snacks, water, and sunscreen and they were on their way. "Wow. It really is green," Madison said. "Almost turquoise." The bright sun bouncing off the water along with a slight breeze caused glimmering slivers of gold on the surface. Madison was glad she brought her sunglasses.

Ali dug into her backpack and extracted two ball caps. "I brought this to protect your pretty head." She handed one to Madison and slipped the other on her own head.

"How does it look," Madison asked, tilting her head from side to side.

"Gorgeous. Oh. You mean the hat? It's okay." She took Madison's hand and led her to the nearest trail.

The trees were in their full glory, leaves gently swaying in the warm spring air. Thin rays of sunshine filtered through the branches here and there and opened to the full glory of the sun in other spots. "Would you like to sit and enjoy the water for a bit?" Ali asked as they came to a clearing. A well-worn wooden bench sat by the edge of the water.

"It is a beautiful spot. Is all of Syracuse this beautiful?" They sat and she closed her eyes, tilting her face toward the sun.

"Syracuse is so diverse. There are some rough spots in the city, nice suburbs, and wonderful parks like this one. We have a great sports stadium and the Dome. I just wish there was more sun." And more of that small-town feel, Ali thought. Like in Clyde.

"What are you talking about? The sun is perfect."

Ali laughed. "Today it is. But Syracuse is one of the cloudiest cities in the US. So, we tend to enjoy it more when it does show its face."

Madison turned toward Ali. "Do you ever miss Clyde?"

Ali didn't even have to think about it. When she first left, she couldn't get away fast enough. The small town that had once held her life felt like living in hell when her heart shattered. She only saw its lack then—lack of diversity, lack of culture, lack of anything interesting, lack of Madison's heart. Syracuse seemed like a whole different universe with all it had to offer in comparison. "I do." It was a simple answer but held a world of meaning. She wasn't sure if it was because Clyde had changed or because she had. Probably both. It was also the home of the woman she cared so much about. How could any place be better than that?

"You know what this spot would be good for?" Madison asked.

"What?"

"Making out." Madison wiggled her eyebrows.

"It is," Ali started. "But we may not be alone. Do you care if someone sees us?"

"I am not nearly as small town as I seem—or used to be. I don't care if the whole world sees us. They would probably be jealous because I will be kissing the prettiest woman in town, maybe even the whole state."

"Then what are you waiting for? Get those lips over here."

Madison didn't hesitate, she took Ali's face in her hands and planted a light kiss on her lips. The second kiss was much deeper and longer.

Ali parted her lips to let Madison's insistent tongue have its way with her. Electricity surged through her. They were panting when they finally came up for air. If anyone had walked by and seen them, Ali had no idea. She had been too wrapped up in Madison to notice.

"Well, that was nice," Ali said.

"Just nice? I must not have been doing it right." She went in for round two with more voraciousness.

"If it gets any better than that I'm not going to be able to control myself." If there was one thing Madison was excellent at it was kissing. But there were so many things Madison excelled at. Too many for Ali to count.

"Is that bad?"

"Only if you mind being naked in public."

Madison seemed to think about it for a beat. "Kissing in public is fine. Not so sure I want to be naked. Although I have had dreams about it."

"That's a coincidence, because I have too."

"I think dreams about being naked in public are common," Madison said.

"No, I wasn't talking about me being naked. I've dreamt about you naked—in public—in private. It doesn't matter as long as you're naked in the dream." Ali laughed.

Madison smacked her on the arm but joined in the laughter. Her face lit up and Ali's heart melted.

They sat there for a while longer, enjoying the sunshine, the view, and each other. "Ready?" Ali asked. "We should probably get going if we are going to get dinner and have you on your way on time."

"What are we going to do when I go home?" Madison asked. Was that a bit of sadness in her voice?

"What do you want to do? Besides sexting?"

"What do you know about sexting?"

"Nothing, but I'm willing to google it."

Madison scrunched up her face. "Somehow that doesn't seem like it would be enough."

Ali took her hand. "I'm coming down in a few weeks. Until then, we text, we talk, we Facetime."

Madison laid her head on Ali's shoulder. "Guess that will have to do. For now."

Dinner and the rest of the day went by way too fast. It was almost seven when Ali kissed Madison good-bye and watched her drive away. She felt empty before Madison was even out of sight.

Her phone rang as if on cue. "I thought you were going to call me as soon as Madison left."

"You called her Madison." Ali headed back inside to her apartment.

"That's her name isn't it?"

"You usually call her by her first *and* last name."

"That's before she was a real person. I feel like I know her now."

"What did you think of her? Truthfully."

"Oh, honey, when have I ever been anything but honest—and blunt?"

"Good point."

"I liked her. She's a keeper."

"I like her too."

"I could see that."

"It shows?" Ali asked.

"Baby, you were glowing like you were on fire. When are you going to see her again?"

Not soon enough. Ali missed her already. How stupid was that. They had spent twenty years apart and Ali had survived— somehow, now she didn't want to be without her for even a day. Ali filled Charley in on their future plans. "After that I'm not sure. Seems like we'll be doing the long-distance thing for a while." Not Ali's favorite idea. But what choice did they have?

"I'm happy for you, sweetie," Charley said.

"Thank you. And thank you for insisting I contact my exes. Without you I wouldn't have reconnected with Madison. I don't think I can ever adequately repay you."

"Yes, you can. I'll think of something. I'll be sure to let you know when I do. Maybe a new car."

"I love you," Ali said.

"Just remember one thing."

"What's that?"

"Pink is my favorite color."

She went into her office as soon as they hung up and opened her laptop. The sooner she got her rewrites done, the sooner she could go to Clyde.

CHAPTER NINETEEN

Madison poured coffee into Joe's cup. "I'm so glad you two convinced me to hear Ali out, although I was still pretty angry with her when I did."

"So, what changed?" Tom asked.

"I was reminded of who she is. The more time we spent together, the more I saw it. I fought it. Scared I guess."

"That's understandable," Joe said. "Given some of your history."

"I was scared when I first started dating Joe," Tom said.

"You were?" Joe asked him. "Why? Was it because we had to hide our relationship?"

"No. It was because you were so good looking. I was afraid I would pale in comparison."

"Oh, you are so full of crap, old man."

"I love you guys," Madison said. They were the perfect example of what she hoped to have with Ali.

"We love you too, sweetie." Tom said. "So, it's going well with Ali?"

"It is. We've been talking one way or another every day since I got back from Syracuse. She should be here sometime tomorrow. I can't wait to see her." She never knew two weeks could seem so long. "How did you guys do it?"

"Do what?"

"Stay together for so long, even when the world didn't think you should?"

"Love, my darling. Love," Joe said.

Tom nodded his agreement.

Love. Could it really be that simple?

"And trust and honesty and respect and never going to bed angry and on and on and on. Love is the foundation. Everything else is built on top of that," Joe added.

"And humor and together time and…" Tom said.

"I think she gets the point," Joe said.

"I do," Madison said. "It's not some magic thing that just happens. You have to build it and allow it to grow. Tend it like a garden."

"And just like a garden, it grows. Now that, my dear, *is* magic." Joe leaned over and kissed Tom on the cheek.

Madison looked up as the bell on the door chimed, letting her know someone had come into the shop. She was surprised and happy to see Ali standing there.

"I hear you have the best chocolate cream donuts in town," Ali said.

Tom turned around. "Speak of the devil."

"Who called me a devil?" Ali asked. "Not that I don't deserve that title." She made her way up to the counter.

"What are you doing here?" Madison asked. "You said you weren't coming till tomorrow."

"Oh, crap. Am I early? This isn't Wednesday? I can go and come back tomorrow if you want."

"Come here and give me a kiss, you fool. I'm so happy to see you."

Ali leaned over the counter and kissed Madison gently on the lips. "I missed you. I couldn't stay away any longer."

Madison introduced her to Tom and Joe. "We've heard a lot about you," Joe said. "Nice to actually meet you." Joe put out his hand.

"Do we have to be so formal?" Ali asked. "Can I hug you? I understand you convinced Madison to talk to me."

"We do hugs," Joe said. They each hugged her in turn. Madison seemed downright giddy. "I'm so happy to see you."

"You said that already," Ali said.

"It's worth repeating. Do you want some coffee, a donut, another kiss?"

"Coffee would be great."

"No kiss?" Madison pretended to pout.

"Oh. I thought I only got one from that list."

"And you chose coffee?"

"I figured I would need the caffeine to make sure I stay awake." Ali put the side of her hand up to her mouth as if she were sharing a secret. "For later when we're alone."

Madison shook her head. "You need caffeine in order to stay awake with me?"

"Hey. It was a long drive." Ali gave her attention to the two men at the counter. "I'm just teasing her. I would stay awake for a month for this beautiful woman." She slipped around to the back of the counter, put her arms around Madison's waist, and pulled her in for a kiss.

"I'm so happy to see you too, by the way." She kissed her again.

"Want some help? Where's my apron?" Ali asked.

"No. Sit. I'll get you coffee and a donut. You must be tired after that drive." She disappeared into the back.

Ali did as she was told. She *was* tired. The drive was long, and she had left her apartment early to try to beat some of the traffic—and because she couldn't wait to see Madison again.

"You know Madison has been walking on air since the two of you got back together. I hope you treat her right. She's one special lady," Joe said in a low voice.

"I know. I'm blessed to have her back in my life. I don't ever plan on letting her go again. You have nothing to worry about." She gave them her best reassuring smile.

"Good, because I'd hate to have to yank your liver out through your throat," Tom said. A long beat went by before he burst out laughing.

"What's so funny." Madison was back, carrying a full pot of coffee and a chocolate cream donut.

"Tom's trying to scare the crap out of your lady here," Joe said.

"Tom." Madison raised one eyebrow.

"It's fine," Ali said. "I didn't need my liver anyway."

"Tom," Madison repeated.

"Just funning her a little. You can keep your body parts." Tom winked at Ali.

"All good to hear," Ali said to Madison.

Madison set the donut on a napkin in front of Ali and poured her a cup of coffee. "Do you want to hang out here and watch me work or I can give you the key and you can go to my house until I'm done here. I may be able to get Valerie to come in early so I can leave early."

"I could use a nap. But I would rather sit here and watch you work."

"Don't be silly. Drink your coffee and then go take a nap. I'll let you know later if I can get off early."

"Is that an order? Please make it an order." That nap was sounding more like a necessity than a luxury.

"Yes, it's an order."

As much as she hated to leave Madison, she really did need to get some sleep. Besides getting up early, she'd gone to bed late, rushing to finish her book edits. She drank half of her coffee and wrapped the donut in the napkin to take with her. She said her good-byes, kissed Madison again, and headed to Madison's house. She was asleep within minutes of lying down on the couch.

She jumped when she heard the front door close. She hadn't heard it open. "Ali?" Madison whispered. Ali didn't say anything. Her eyes were still closed as she tried to figure out how long she'd been asleep and why Madison didn't text to say she was coming home. Madison came around the side of the couch and leaned closer. "Ali," she whispered again.

Without warning, Ali opened her eyes, grabbed Madison, and pulled her down. Madison nearly toppled over and ended up on top of Ali, with her feet still on the floor. "Hey."

"I missed you." Ali planted little kisses along her jawline.

"You scared me."

"Sorry." Ali laughed.

Madison tickled her ribs. "I can tell how sorry you are." Madison sat up on the edge of the couch. "Tom and Joe were impressed with you."

"Why? Did you brag about me? Tell them I'm a best-selling author and all? Tell them how smart I am?"

Madison laughed. "You're strange. Did anyone ever tell you that?"

"All the time. I can't believe you're just now seeing it." Ali sat up and pulled Madison back until she was leaning against Ali. Ali wrapped her arms around her. It felt so good to hold her.

"Oh, I've known it for years. I just never mentioned it before. I did *not* tell them any of that stuff, although I have been kind of bending their ears about you for a couple of weeks now. No. They liked that you could take a joke."

"Yeah. That threat to pull my liver out? That was a joke? He seemed so serious."

"If it helps any, I did give him permission to do it, if you done do me wrong."

"Done do me wrong? Have you been listening to country music again?"

"Maybe."

"I like them too. They seem like good guys, and they sure do care about you. That makes them okay in my book."

"Your *New York Times* best-selling book?"

Ali laughed. "I'm not the only strange one around here."

"I know. That's why we make a good pair."

Ali tilted Madison's chin and kissed her. "I like that. I like you. I like being here." Here with Madison. Here in Clyde.

"I like you being here." Madison kissed her back. "I sent you a text by the way saying I was on my way. You must have slept through it. My poor tired baby."

"I'm awake now." She put her head on Madison's shoulder and pretended to snore.

"Do you need to sleep more?" Madison asked.

Ali picked her head back up. "No way. I'm just teasing. I want to spend time with you, not sleep."

Madison lifted herself from the couch and put her hand out to Ali. "Come in the kitchen with me. Keep me company while I make us dinner." Ali grasped her hand and let Madison pull her up. Madison poured a glass of water and set it on the island for Ali. "Sit. Relax." She opened the fridge and pulled out a head of cauliflower. She grabbed a cutting board and a chef's knife from the wooden block on the counter.

"I should be doing that. You worked all day."

"I repeat. Sit. Relax. You drove all day. Let me do this for you."

Ali sat on one of the barstools lining the side of the island. "Thank you."

"You cooked for me the whole time my back was out. This is the least I can do."

"Never let it be said that you didn't do the least you could do." Ali chuckled.

Madison flashed her a perfect smile. "I missed you so much."

"Ditto."

Madison stopped what she was doing and turned her full attention to Ali. "Ali, I don't just mean the past couple of weeks. I mean the last twenty years. I didn't realize how much until you came back into my life. There was a void there. I couldn't quite figure out what it was. What that empty feeling was. Now I know it was the lack of you. Does that make sense?"

Ali knew that feeling well. She hadn't known what it was either. She tried to fill it with people that didn't fit. "It does. I feel the same."

"My soul longed for something. That something was you."

Ali's eyes filled with unexpected tears. "You've got me now. I'm sorry for the huge canyon I caused between us for so long. Madison, I'm not going anywhere. We are going to get what we always wanted. Together. I promise."

Madison came around the corner of the island and wrapped her arms around Ali. Ali felt like she belonged there, in those arms. "I make you the same promise, Ali."

"Are we crazy?"

Madison pulled back and looked in Ali's eyes. "Crazy how?"

"We haven't been back in each other's lives that long."

"Are you having doubts?"

"That's the crazy part. I'm not."

"Do you think you should?" Madison went back to chopping the cauliflower.

"If it was anyone else but you, yeah, I would be questioning the hell out of how fast I've fallen." Ali took a drink of her water. All this emotion was making her throat dry.

"Don't you think our history plays into it?"

"It has to. It's the only thing that makes sense."

Madison scraped the cauliflower pieces into a large bowl. "You always were the cerebral one between the two of us. I run more on emotion."

"Believe me, you've brought out the emotion in me. Are you saying I'm overthinking this?"

"No. It's just you, being you."

"It is crazy. You're crazy. I'm crazy. So, I say let's be crazy together."

"That sounds like a plan to me," Madison said.

"Do you need a plan?" *Did* they need a plan? Should they just keep going like they were for a while longer? Could they? Were either one of them ready to make a commitment? The promises they'd just made were a commitment. Weren't they? So many questions ran through Ali's mind before she even gave Madison a chance to answer.

Madison took her time thinking it over. "No. I am happy to take it day by day. Which for me is uncommon. I usually like to know what to expect, what's going to happen next. Do you?"

"I don't think so. As long as I know the next time I'll be seeing you, that's all I need. I just don't want too much time to pass between our visits."

"Me either." Madison chopped a clove of garlic and added it to the bowl.

"I was thinking…"

"See. There you go thinking again."

"What would you say if I got an apartment here in town?"

"You don't want to stay with me?"

Ali shook her head. "No, that's not it at all. What if I have a part-time home here? That way I can spend more time in Clyde without invading your space. I could go back and forth between Syracuse and here and have an apartment in both places."

"I love the idea of you being here more. And I never feel like you are invading my space. I like having you around. It felt good to come home and have you here. If you're worried about having a place to work, I've got three bedrooms. One is just being used for storage. We can clean it out and make you an office."

Ali rolled the idea around in her head. She could work on her writing when Madison was at O's working. Would Madison get sick of having her around like her other ex-girlfriends had? Madison wasn't like any of the other women she had dated. And she was different when she was with Madison as well. She was more herself. She allowed herself to be more of herself because Madison wanted her just the way she was. "Are you sure?"

"Ali, I wouldn't have suggested it if I had any doubts."

"It wouldn't be all the time. I'm thinking maybe two weeks here, two weeks in Syracuse."

"Stop trying to sell me on the idea. I've already emptied that room out in my mind and bought new curtains and a desk for you. All you have to do is accept my offer and bring your computer."

"And clothes."

"Oh. I was hoping you worked naked." Madison added a few more things to the bowl and gave it a good stir.

"You wish."

"I do."

"You're so bad."

"I thought you liked it when I'm bad."

"I do."

Madison laughed. "What's your answer?"

"What was the question?"

"Oh my God, woman. Keep track of the conversation here."

"Sorry. I got distracted with the thought of you being bad." She closed her eyes and tilted her chin up. "Oh, so bad."

"The question was, will you stay here? If your heart is set on your own apartment, I won't object. I may cry a little, but I won't object. I really would like to have you here."

"I don't seem to have a choice. I don't want to make you cry. If it gets too much having me here, you need to let me know."

"Trust me, it won't."

That was the exact reason Ali agreed to Madison's proposition. Trust. She trusted her. What's more, she trusted herself more now than she ever did. "Yay." Madison tried to play it cool and keep her excitement from bubbling over and making her look like a silly schoolgirl. She couldn't help but clap her hands together. "Yay," she repeated. She spread the cauliflower mixture out on a cookie sheet and slid it into the oven. "Shit." She realized that she had been so caught up in their conversation that she forgot to turn the oven on.

"You forgot to light the oven, didn't you?"

"Get out of my head. How did you know that?"

"I've been watching you. I was quite impressed with your knife skills—as well as a little frightened."

Madison removed the cookie sheet and turned the oven on. "Dinner will be a little later than originally planned."

"Can we make out while the oven is heating up, because watching you is heating me up."

"You want to act like a couple of teenagers?"

"Sure. We have a lot of time to make up for. And there's no time like the present to start."

CHAPTER TWENTY

Charley helped Ali put the last box in the car. "What am I going to do without you, baby doll?" he moaned.

"I'm only going to be gone for two weeks. I'll be back. We'll talk." Ali was looking forward to her first two full weeks in Clyde with Madison.

"You'll be back, then you'll be gone again. And we both know this is only temporary." He flung his head to the side dramatically, flinging a hunk of bright green hair with it.

"Only temporary?"

"Girl, you are crazy about that woman. You miss her something wicked when you're here and she's there."

"Yes."

"It won't be long before you move there permanently. You are going to leave and forget all about me."

"I could never forget you. And no matter what happens with Madison, you're still my guy, slash girl, slash best friend."

Charley threw his arms around Ali. "I'm going to miss you. Don't forget to write?"

"Write? Like an actual letter?"

"No. Your next book. Don't get too distracted. I've met Madison. She can be very distracting. If she was my girl I would just sit and look at her all day."

Ali laughed. She had to agree, Madison was beautiful. "I'll do my best."

"That's all I ask. Oh, and yeah, write me a letter now and then. Will ya?"

"How about I call?" Ali ran her packing list through her head to see if she was forgetting anything. She shut her trunk, gave Charley a hug, and was on her way. It wasn't completely a new life, but it was certainly an adventure. One she was looking forward to. A hundred miles outside of Clyde, she pulled into a rest stop and googled pet stores. There was one in Clyde when she was growing up, but she noticed the building now housed a hardware store. She found what she was looking for and put the address in her GPS. Once her mission there was complete, she continued to Madison's house. She wanted to get everything unloaded before Madison finished her shift at O's. She found a note taped to Madison's door.

My dearest Ali,

I want you to think of this as your home. I am excited to share it with you. I've cleared out half of the closet and the dresser in the corner for you. As promised, you have a brand-new desk and curtains in your new office. I also got you an office chair. I know that is a personal thing and needs to fit your cute little butt just right. So, I saved the receipt in case you want to exchange it. I made you lunch. It's in the Tupperware bowl on the top shelf in the fridge. Three minutes in the microwave and it should be good to go. There is a chocolate cream donut on the counter for you in the Ziploc bag. I'll be home (our home) around five. I can't wait to see you.

Madison

The note brought tears to Ali's eyes. She spent a whole lot of years living in a cocoon, not really feeling emotions. She had cried so many times since coming back to Clyde. Something in between not feeling and blubbering like an idiot would be nice.

She took the box of things she had purchased at the pet store and set up a large fishbowl with a filter, gravel, a few plastic plants, and a fake neon green cave. She filled the bowl with water, set it on the kitchen counter, and followed the directions to take out the chlorine and introduce the goldfish safely to its new home, just like the guy at the pet store had instructed her.

In the fridge went the bottle of champagne she'd brought and out came the lunch Madison made her. A few fresh tears rolled down her cheeks. Damn it. What a wimp, crying over meatloaf.

Ali finished her lunch and brought her clothes and laptop upstairs. She was touched by all the work and thought that Madison had put into her new office. Fresh flowers sat on top of a bookcase against the wall, and brand-new copies of her books sat on one of its shelves. "No more tears," she told herself.

She sat in the office chair. Obviously expensive. It was perfect. She turned around and took in the framed pictures on the wall. Most were art prints, but one was of her and Madison as teenagers, their arms wrapped around each other, a huge smile on both of their faces. Ali was sure her smile now was just as big. Perfect. Everything was perfect.

She was just finishing up a chapter when she heard Madison come into the house. She closed her laptop and headed down to greet her. One hug and three kisses later, they sat down on the couch together.

"You went above and beyond with my office. I love it," Ali said.

"I'm glad. Were you able to get any work done today?"

Ali gave her a quick rundown on the progress for her newest book. "My detective is getting a girlfriend in this book. It's time."

The smile on Madison's face told Ali she approved. "Art imitating life?"

"Something like that."

"What do you like best and dislike about writing?" It was so nice having Ali back and knowing she wouldn't be leaving again in two or three days. They had two wonderful weeks to spend together this time.

"Hmm. It's hard sometimes. I don't like that."

"What's the hardest part?"

"Getting my ass in the chair to do it."

"I can understand that. If I didn't have an actual schedule for the donut shop, I could see myself blowing off work," Madison said. "What do you like about it?"

"I like that it will live on after I do. My books will be out there in the world even when I'm not." Madison gave it a moment's thought. "That must be a good feeling. I don't have anything to leave behind."

Ali gave her a kiss on the top of her nose. "That's not true. You have the love from your family and a famous donut legacy. Your love, your family, your friends, your donuts, they all mean something in this world."

"Why are we talking about dying? I want to talk about living."

"You started it." Ali laughed. "By the way, thank you for lunch. The meatloaf made me cry."

"What? Was it bad?" Madison had made it the night before, knowing it was one of Ali's favorites.

"No. It was perfect. I'm just a blubbering baby these days. It's like my emotions have decided to hang out on the surface."

"Did you cry when you saw the picture of us as teenagers that I hung on your wall?" Madison had spent half of her day off going through old boxes until she found the picture she was looking for.

"No. That one made me smile."

Madison tilted her head. "Wait. You cry over meatloaf, but not over a sentimental picture like that?"

"I know. Right? I'm all kinds of messed up."

"It's my fault isn't it?"

"Damn right it is, woman."

"What can I do to make it right?"

Ali seemed to think for a beat. "You're going to have to kiss me. It may be the only thing that helps."

Madison was more than happy to oblige. After a few minutes of some heavy kissing and light petting, they came up for air. "How was that? Do you feel any better?"

"A little. I think I need some more."

"Whatever it takes to cure you." She leaned in for another round. Her body responded as Ali's tongue entered her mouth and she pulled back. "If we keep this up, I'm going to have my way with you right here on the couch."

"And that's a problem, why?"

"Because I have a special dinner planned for you. I want to see if T-bone steak makes you cry." She stood up and pulled Ali up with her.

"You're so funny," Ali deadpanned.

"That's why you like me."

"That's just one reason of many."

"I need to light the grill. You can pour us some wine if you want."

"I want."

Madison looked at Ali. She wanted too, but it wasn't wine she craved. She shook the thought from her brain and headed through the kitchen on her way out to the deck, with Ali on her heels. She stopped in her tracks. "What's this?" She pointed to the fishbowl.

"That's Henry, our new goldfish. I didn't want you to be lonely when I'm not here."

"Henry?"

"Yep. That's what he said his name is. I suppose you can change it if you want. But he probably won't come when you call him, if you do."

"Hi, Henry." Madison bent down and looked at him through the glass. "I love him," she said to Ali.

"He loves you too. I can tell by the way he is opening and closing his mouth."

Madison gave Ali a hug. "Thank you." She finished her trek to the deck and the grill. The faster they got through with dinner, the faster they could head upstairs, and Madison could thank Ali properly for her gift.

The two weeks seemed to fly by, and it was time for Ali to leave for Syracuse again. She had less to take home than she had brought with her, leaving clothes and some personal items at Madison's.

They stood in the driveway by Ali's car with their arms around each other. "I don't want to let you go," Madison said.

"I know. I feel the same. I'll call you tomorrow on your lunch break. And I'll be back in two weeks."

"Text me when you get home. I don't care that it will be late."

"I will."

Ali gave her a long kiss. "I'll miss you," she said.

With great difficulty, she let Madison go, got into her car, and headed in the direction of Syracuse. She gave Madison one last wave. She could see Madison in her rearview mirror until she turned the corner and was out of sight. It had been a wonderful two weeks. She couldn't remember the last time she laughed that much or made love that often. They had gotten together with Madison's family a few times, and Grayson let it be known that she was his buddy for life. It was cute the way he would run to her and climb up on her lap. It felt so good to be a part of Madison's life again.

Her apartment seemed so empty when she walked in and turned on the lights. "Hello," she said. "I'm home." She could almost hear her voice echo back to her. After she sent Madison a quick text, she got herself ready for bed and climbed under the cold sheets. Alone.

They went on like this for three months. Each time Ali left to go home it got harder and harder. And her apartment got lonelier and lonelier. Having Charley over much of the time helped, but it didn't stop her from longing for Madison. "I was thinking of coming a few days early if that's okay with you," Ali said to Madison over the phone.

"Of course, it's okay with me. That's great. When are you coming?"

"Fifteen minutes?"

"What?" Madison asked.

Ali looked at her GPS. "I'm about fifteen minutes from O's."

"I've got a chocolate cream donut with your name on it. I can't wait to see you."

"I want more than a chocolate cream donut."

"I've got vanilla cream too."

"I want you. Naked. On the couch. On the floor. On the bed. Anywhere and everywhere."

"Ditto. I can't go into more detail because I'm at work." Ali could almost hear the blush in Madison's voice.

"Of course. Should I tell you what I want to do to you once I have you naked?" Ali could only guess what their conversation was doing to Madison because it was making her wet. She clenched her thighs together against the feeling.

"Um. I would, but I don't think I can handle that right now. Did I mention that I'm at work?"

"Are you in your office?"

"No. I'm in the shop. Valerie is on break and Lea's waiting on customers."

Ali turned on her blinker and moved over so she could get off at exit nineteen. She didn't really need her GPS to get her to Clyde anymore. She used it more out of habit. "Oh, so telling you that I want to lick—"

"Ali, can you save this. I really want to hear it, but not at this moment."

Ali smiled. "Sure. How about I show you later?"

"That sounds good. I've got to go. I'll see you soon."

"Bye, baby."

Just as she promised, Madison had her favorite donut ready when she arrived. Ali had to settle for a kiss on the check. O's was full. Valerie was back from her break, and both she and Lea were busy taking orders and delivering food to tables while Madison manned the cash register. Ali offered to help, but Madison turned her down. "Relax. You had a long drive. Do you want anything to eat or drink, besides that donut?"

"Nope. I'm fine. Go do what you've got to do. Are you done at five today?"

"Yeah. You can head to the house if you don't want to wait."

Ali was more than happy to just sit there, enjoy her donut, and watch Madison work. "I'll stay till you're done." Madison gave her another kiss on the cheek and went over to wait on a customer who had just sat down at the counter. It wasn't long before she hung up her apron and was done for the day. They stopped back at Madison's house so she could change out of her work clothes. Ali didn't mind that she smelled like jelly donuts, but Madison didn't seem to like it. Ali insisted on taking her out to dinner and Madison readily agreed.

"I'm so glad you came early. I missed you," Madison said as they waited for their dinner. "Henry did too."

Ali sipped her wine. It felt good to relax with Madison after her long drive and Madison's long workday. "I missed you too."

"Not Henry?" Madison aked.

"I Facetime with Henry almost every day while you're at work, so not so much. I'm surprised he never mentioned it to you."

"I am too. That little shit seems to be keeping secrets. How is your book coming along?"

"Good. It's been flowing easily. I used to think the only way I could write was from heartache and hurt. Turns out I write faster from being happy."

"I'm so glad to hear that. And to hear that you're happy."

"How can I be anything but happy with you as my woman?"

"Good point."

"And Charley?"

"He's not my woman."

Madison laughed. "I would hope not. How is he doing? He must miss you when you're here."

"He does. But lately I barely see him when I'm home—I mean back in Syracuse. I'm thinking of Clyde more and more as home. Anyway, he's fine. Got a promotion at work. He's the manager of the makeup department now. If there's anything that makes him happy, it's makeup."

"That's wonderful."

"He also met someone. They've been going out for a couple of months now."

"Male or female?" Madison asked. "Wait. I know now there are other choices. I'm not sure how to phrase the question."

Ali smiled. "That's okay. Male. All male. He seems like a really good guy. Charley is head over heels."

"Oh, I'm so glad. He deserves someone nice."

Ali couldn't agree more. Besides being happy for Charley, it also helped her feel less like she was abandoning him when she was in Clyde. Madison filled Ali in on the newest happenings in Clyde while they ate. Not that there were very many.

Ali paid the check and they headed back to Madison's house. They were barely in the door when Ali pulled Madison close. She found Madison's mouth with hers and kissed her completely and thoroughly. "I've wanted to do that all day."

"What took you so long?"

"Good things come to those that can't kiss their girlfriend like that in public."

Madison laughed. "I'm pretty sure that's not how the quote goes."

"Close enough. Would you think me rude if I suggested we go upstairs right now?"

"I'd think you were hot and sexy if you suggest that."

"Then that's what I suggest."

They wasted no time making their way to the bedroom. Ali slipped her hands under Madison's blouse and drank in the feeling of her silky-smooth skin. It was intoxicating. Madison undid the buttons on her shirt and let it fall to the floor. She took Ali's face in her hands and kissed her deeply. Ali helped her slip out of her pants and underwear without breaking the contact of their lips.

Ali's insides were on fire. She broke the kiss long enough for Madison to help her out of her clothes. The only thing standing in the way of their bodies becoming one, as they stood in each other's arms, was Madison's sports bra. Ali pulled the offending fabric and lifted it over Madison's head and tossed it on the pile of clothes on the floor. She pushed her back onto the bed and in an instant was on top of her. Ali's hands were in her hair, her lips on her mouth, her neck, her breasts. She hungrily sucked a nipple into her mouth and heard Madison moan. The sound sent a rush of moisture between Ali's legs and urged her on. She bathed each breast in turn with her tongue and was rewarded with more titillating sounds from deep within Madison. She took her time working her way down Madison's body, kissing, licking, and teasing along the way. Madison's fingers were weaved through her hair guiding her to the spot she desired.

"You're so wet," Ali said, slipping a finger through Madison's slick folds.

"That started as soon as you kissed me," Madison groaned. Her legs trembled as Ali pushed them farther apart gaining her better access to Madison's most sacred place, and she sucked in a loud breath as Ali's tongue swept across her flesh. Ali reveled in the sounds and reactions she was eliciting from Madison, and her own body reacted in kind. It didn't take long before the waves of an orgasm overtook Madison and Ali stopped her movements but increased the pressure of her tongue. She gave her a minute to come down from the ride, crawled up beside her and pulled her into her arms. "Did I mention that I missed you?"

Ali surmised that Madison was having trouble talking, because she only nodded, and snuggled deeper into Ali's arm. Madison's heartbeat was so strong that Ali could feel it against her own chest. It had barely reached a normal rate when Madison raked the back of her fingernails across Ali's breasts and followed the return path with her fingertips. Ali's nipples hardened under her touch. Madison walked her fingers down Ali's body and slid them through the wetness waiting for her there. Ali's breath caught in her throat. Madison slid first one finger, then two into her and rubbed her thumb against Ali's clit. Ali lifted her hips upward, pressing herself harder against Madison's expertly moving hand. She felt lightheaded as her orgasm approached. She tried to hold it off and at the same time, she yearned for it. She lost the battle as an orgasm ripped through her and bright lights seemed to flash behind her tightly closed eyes.

Madison slowed the rhythm of her fingers, drawing out the orgasm, until the sensation became too great and Ali had to pull her hand away. She pulled Madison up next to her and held her tight. The throbbing between her legs matched the beating of her heart. It took a few minutes to settle back down. "I can't keep doing this," Madison said.

Ali was confused. "Doing what? Having sex with me?" Her heart sank. Was Madison breaking up with her? She couldn't survive losing her again.

"No, silly. I love having sex with you. I love *you*."

Ali hadn't dare say those words, even though she'd felt it. She wanted to give Madison time to get there as well. "I love you, too. I always have."

Madison kissed her gently on the mouth. "I can't keep saying good-bye to you and being away from you. I want you to move back here permanently. You can live here, or if you don't want that we can sell this house and buy another one. A house that's *ours*."

Ali pulled back to look at her. It wasn't like she hadn't had similar thoughts. Dreamt of it. But she wasn't about to invite herself to live with Madison. But now Madison was doing the inviting. That was a whole different story.

"What do you think? Please say yes."

"Yes."

"Yes? For real?" Her excitement seemed to bubble over.

"Yes. Wait till I tell Henry that his parents will be living together, like a real family. He will be so happy."

"Oh, Ali. I'm so happy."

Madison kissed her hard, starting a whole new wave of passion and another round of lovemaking.

EPILOGUE

Ali sat in her favorite booth waiting for her lunch order so she could get back to her writing and the house she and Madison bought together four months ago. She loved being back in Clyde and loved living with Madison even more. She missed Charley of course, but they talked almost every day, and Charley was planning on a trip down to visit soon. His boyfriend had moved in after only three months of dating. Just your typical *lesbian*, Ali had teased him.

Madison handed a bag of food to Ali, leaned over the counter, and gave her a kiss. "Thanks, baby."

"See you at home, later. Geez, I like saying that." Madison smiled.

Ali turned to go and almost ran right into Tilly Miller.

"Well," Tilly said. "I see what's going on here. I never pegged you for one of *those*."

"Those what?" Madison asked her.

"You know darn well. One of those *lesbians*, just like you."

"That's right," Ali said. "And guess what? I ended up with the head cheerleader. Everyone in high school had a crush on her. You probably did too."

"Well, I never," Tilly said in a huff.

"You should. It might improve your disposition," Madison said. "Here, I'll cash you out." She reached for the bill in Tilly's hand. "Oh yeah, you got the tuna melt on rye. Did you know that is a favorite among lesbians? Does Ross know you lean that way?"

Tilly threw a twenty-dollar bill on the counter and turned to leave without another word. "Don't you want your change," Madison called after her. She continued her trek out the door without turning around.

"I can't believe you just did that," Ali said.

"She insulted my girlfriend. I don't want people like that in here."

"She called me a lesbian. That's hardly an insult."

"It's the way she said it. Like it's a dirty word."

"Have I told you lately that I love you?" Ali asked.

"You told me this morning, but you can tell me again."

"I love you."

"I love you too." They were words that held so much meaning. Words they said to each other when they were young. Words that Ali would never tire of saying or hearing now that they were adults and had somehow found each other again. Words that Ali planned on saying for the rest of her life.

About the Author

Creativity for Joy Argento started young. She was only five, growing up in Syracuse, New York, when she picked up a pencil and began drawing animals. These days she calls Rochester home, and oil paints are her medium of choice. Her award-winning art has found its way into homes around the globe.

Writing came later in life for Joy. Her love of lesbian romance inspired her to try her hand at writing, and she found her first self-published novels well received. She is thrilled to be a part of the Bold Strokes family and has enjoyed their books for years.

Joy has three grown children who are making their own way in the world and four grandsons who are the light of her life.

Visit her website at www.joyargento.com.

Books Available from Bold Strokes Books

#shedeservedit by Greg Herren. When his gay best friend, and high school football star, is murdered, Alex Wheeler is a suspect and must find the truth to clear himself. (978-1-63555-996-5)

Always by Kris Bryant. When a pushy American private investigator shows up demanding to meet the woman in Camila's artwork, instead of introducing her to her great-grandmother, Camila decides to lead her on a wild goose chase all over Italy. (978-1-63679-027-5)

Exes and O's by Joy Argento. Ali and Madison really only have one thing in common. The girl who broke their heart may be the only one who can put it back together. (978-1-63679-017-6)

One Verse Multi by Sander Santiago. Life was good: promotion, friends, falling in love, discovering that the multi-verse is on a fast track to collision—wait, what? Good thing Martin King works for a company that can fix the problem, right…um…right? (978-1-63679-069-5)

Paris Rules by Jaime Maddox. Carly Becker has been searching for the perfect woman all her life, but no one ever seems to be just right until Paige Waterford checks all her boxes, except the most important one—she's married. (978-1-63679-077-0)

Shadow Dancers by Suzie Clarke. In this third and final book in the Moon Shadow series, Rachel must find a way to become the hunter and not the hunted, and this time she will meet Ehsee Yumiko head-on. (978-1-63555-829-6)

The Kiss by C.A. Popovich. When her wife refuses their divorce and begins to stalk her, threatening her life, Kate realizes to protect her new love, Leslie, she has to let her go, even if it breaks her heart. (978-1-63679-079-4)

The Wedding Setup by Charlotte Greene. When Ryann, a big-time New York executive, goes to Colorado to help out with her best friend's wedding, she never expects to fall for the maid of honor. (978-1-63679-033-6)

Velocity by Gun Brooke. Holly and Claire work toward an uncertain future preparing for an alien space mission, and only one thing is for certain, they will have to risk their lives, and their hearts, to discover the truth. (978-1-63555-983-5)

Wildflower Words by Sam Ledel. Lida Jones treks West with her father in search of a better life on the rapidly developing American frontier, but finds home when she meets Hazel Thompson. (978-1-63679-055-8)

A Fairer Tomorrow by Kathleen Knowles. For Maddie Weeks and Gerry Stern, the Second World War brought them together, but the end of the war might rip them apart. (978-1-63555-874-6)

Holiday Hearts by Diana Day-Admire and Lyn Cole. Opposites attract during Christmastime chaos in Kansas City. (978-1-63679-128-9)

Changing Majors by Ana Hartnett Reichardt. Beyond a love, beyond a coming-out, Bailey Sullivan discovers what lies beyond the shame and self-doubt imposed on her by traditional Southern ideals. (978-1-63679-081-7)

Fresh Grave in Grand Canyon by Lee Patton. The age-old Grand Canyon becomes more and more ominous as a group of volunteers fight to survive alone in nature and uncover a murderer among them. (978-1-63679-047-3)

Highland Whirl by Anna Larner. Opposites attract in the Scottish Highlands, when feisty Alice Campbell falls for city-girl-about-town Roxanne Barns. (978-1-63555-892-0)

Humbug by Amanda Radley. With the corporate Christmas party in jeopardy, CEO Rosalind Caldwell hires Christmas Girl Ellie Pearce as her personal assistant. The only problem is, Ellie isn't a PA, has never planned a party, and develops a ridiculous crush on her totally intimidating new boss. (978-1-63555-965-1)

On the Rocks by Georgia Beers. Schoolteacher Vanessa Martini makes no apologies for her dating checklist, and newly single mom Grace Chapman ticks all Vanessa's Do Not Date boxes. Of course, they're never going to fall in love. (978-1-63555-989-7)

Song of Serenity by Brey Willows. Arguing with the Muse of music and justice is complicated, falling in love with her even more so. (978-1-63679-015-2)

The Christmas Proposal by Lisa Moreau. Stranded together in a Christmas village on a snowy mountain, Grace and Bridget face their past and question their dreams for the future. (978-1-63555-648-3)

The Infinite Summer by Morgan Lee Miller. While spending the summer with her dad in a small beach town, Remi Brenner falls for Harper Hebert and accidentally finds herself tangled up in an intense restaurant rivalry between her famous stepmom and her first love. (978-1-63555-969-9)

Wisdom by Jesse J. Thoma. When Sophia and Reggie are chosen for the governor's new community design team and tasked with tackling substance abuse and mental health issues, battle lines are drawn even as sparks fly. (978-1-63555-886-9)

A Convenient Arrangement by Aurora Rey and Jaime Clevenger. Cuffing season has come for lesbians, and for Jess Archer and Cody Dawson, their convenient arrangement becomes anything but. (978-1-63555-818-0)

An Alaskan Wedding by Nance Sparks. The last thing either Andrea or Riley expects is to bump into the one who broke her heart fifteen years ago, but when they meet at the welcome party, their feelings come rushing back. (978-1-63679-053-4)

Beulah Lodge by Cathy Dunnell. It's 1874, and newly engaged Ruth Mallowes is set on marriage and life as a missionary… until she falls in love with the housemaid at Beulah Lodge. (978-1-63679-007-7)

Gia's Gems by Toni Logan. When Lindsey Speyer discovers that popular travel columnist Gia Williams is a complete fake and threatens to expose her, blackmail has never been so sexy. (978-1-63555-917-0)

Holiday Wishes & Mistletoe Kisses by M. Ullrich. Four holidays, four couples, four chances to make their wishes come true. (978-1-63555-760-2)

Love By Proxy by Dena Blake. Tess has a secret crush on her best friend, Sophie, so the last thing she wants is to help Sophie fall in love with someone else, but how can she stand in the way of her happiness? (978-1-63555-973-6)

Loyalty, Love, & Vermouth by Eric Peterson. A comic valentine to a gay man's family of choice, including the ones with cold noses and four paws. (978-1-63555-997-2)

Marry Me by Melissa Brayden. Allison Hale attempts to plan the wedding of the century to a man who could save her family's business, if only she wasn't falling for her wedding planner, Megan Kinkaid. (978-1-63555-932-3)

Pathway to Love by Radclyffe. Courtney Valentine is looking for a woman exactly like Ben—smart, sexy, and not in the market for anything serious. All she has to do is convince Ben that sex-without-strings is the perfect pathway to pleasure. (978-1-63679-110-4)

Sweet Surprise by Jenny Frame. Flora and Mac never thought they'd ever see each other again, but when Mac opens up her barber shop right next to Flora's sweet shop, their connection comes roaring back. (978-1-63679-001-5)

The Edge of Yesterday by CJ Birch. Easton Gray is sent from the future to save humanity from technological disaster. When she's forced to target the woman she's falling in love with, can Easton do what's needed to save humanity? (978-1-63679-025-1)

The Scout and the Scoundrel by Barbara Ann Wright. With unexpected danger surrounding them, Zara and Roni are stuck between duty and survival, with little room for exploring their feelings, especially love. (978-1-63555-978-1)

Bury Me in Shadows by Greg Herren. College student Jake Chapman is forced to spend the summer at his dying grandmother's home and soon finds danger from long-buried family secrets. (978-1-63555-993-4)

Can't Leave Love by Kimberly Cooper Griffin. Sophia and Pru have no intention of falling in love, but sometimes love happens when and where you least expect it. (978-1-636790041-1)

Free Fall at Angel Creek by Julie Tizard. Detective Dee Rawlings and aircraft accident investigator Dr. River Dawson use conflicting methods to find answers when a plane goes missing, while overcoming surprising threats, and discovering an unlikely chance at love. (978-1-63555-884-5)

Love's Compromise by Cass Sellars. For Piper Holthaus and Brook Myers, will professional dreams and past baggage stop two hearts from realizing they are meant for each other? (978-1-63555-942-2)

Not All a Dream by Sophia Kell Hagin. Hester has lost the woman she loved and the world has descended into relentless dark and cold. But giving up will have to wait when she stumbles upon people who help her survive. (978-1-63679-067-1)

Protecting the Lady by Amanda Radley. If Eve Webb had known she'd be protecting royalty, she'd never have taken the job as bodyguard, but as the threat to Lady Katherine's life draws closer, she'll do whatever it takes to save her, and may just lose her heart in the process. (978-1-63679-003-9)

The Secrets of Willowra by Kadyan. A family saga of three women, their homestead called Willowra in the Australian outback, and the secrets that link them all. (978-1-63679-064-0)

Trial by Fire by Carsen Taite. When prosecutor Lennox Roy and public defender Wren Bishop become fierce adversaries in a headline-grabbing arson case, their attraction ignites a passion that leads them both to question their assumptions about the law, the truth, and each other. (978-1-63555-860-9)

Turbulent Waves by Ali Vali. Kai Merlin and Vivien Palmer plan their future together as hostile forces make their own plans to destroy what they have, as well as all those they love. (978-1-63679-011-4)

Unbreakable by Cari Hunter. When Dr. Grace Kendal is forced at gunpoint to help an injured woman, she is dragged into a nightmare where nothing is quite as it seems, and their lives aren't the only ones on the line. (978-1-63555-961-3)

Veterinary Surgeon by Nancy Wheelton. When dangerous drugs are stolen from the veterinary clinic, Mitch investigates and Kay becomes a suspect. As pride and professions clash, love seems impossible. (978-1-63679-043-5)

A Different Man by Andrew L. Huerta. This diverse collection of stories chronicling the challenges of gay life at various ages shines a light on the progress made and the progress still to come. (978-1-63555-977-4)

All That Remains by Sheri Lewis Wohl. Johnnie and Shantel might have to risk their lives—and their love—to stop a werewolf intent on killing. (978-1-63555-949-1)

Beginner's Bet by Fiona Riley. Phenom luxury Realtor Ellison Gamble has everything, except a family to share it with, so when a mix-up brings youthful Katie Crawford into her life, she bets the house on love. (978-1-63555-733-6)

Dangerous Without You by Lexus Grey. Throughout their senior year in high school, Aspen, Remington, Denna, and Raleigh face challenges in life and romance that they never expect. (978-1-63555-947-7)

Desiring More by Raven Sky. In this collection of steamy stories, a rich variety of lovers find themselves desiring more, more from a lover, more from themselves, and more from life. (978-1-63679-037-4)

Jordan's Kiss by Nanisi Barrett D'Arnuck. After losing everything in a fire, Jordan Phelps joins a small lounge band and meets pianist Morgan Sparks, who lights another blaze, this time in Jordan's heart. (978-1-63555-980-4)

Late City Summer by Jeanette Bears. Forced together for her wedding, Emily Stanton and Kate Alessi navigate their lingering passion for one another against the backdrop of New York City and World War II, and a summer romance they left behind. (978-1-63555-968-2)

Love and Lotus Blossoms by Anne Shade. On her path to self-acceptance and true passion, Janesse will risk everything—and possibly everyone—she loves. (978-1-63555-985-9)

Love in the Limelight by Ashley Moore. Marion Hargreaves, the finest actress of her generation, and Jessica Carmichael, the world's biggest pop star, rediscover each other twenty years after an ill-fated affair. (978-1-63679-051-0)

Suspecting Her by Mary P. Burns. Complications ensue when Erin O'Connor falls for top real estate saleswoman Catherine Williams while investigating racism in the real estate industry; the fallout could end their chance at happiness. (978-1-63555-960-6)

Two Winters by Lauren Emily Whalen. A modern YA retelling of Shakespeare's *The Winter's Tale* about birth, death, Catholic school, improv comedy, and the healing nature of time. (978-1-63679-019-0)